CREATURES THAT ONCE WERE MEN

By MAXIM GORKY

Translated from the Russian by J. M. SHIRAZI and Others

Introduction by G. K. CHESTERTON

BONI AND LIVERIGHT, INC.

PUBLISHERS   NEW YORK

Printed in the U. S. A.

CONTENTS

		PAGE
INTRODUCTION	. . . . . .	V
CREATURES THAT ONCE WERE MEN	. .	13
TWENTY-SIX MEN AND A GIRL	. . .	104
CHELKASH	. . . . . .	125
· MY FELLOW-TRAVELLER	. . . .	178
ON A RAFT	. . . . . .	229

INTRODUCTION

By G. K. Chesterton

It is certainly a curious fact that so many of the voices of what is called our modern religion have come from countries which are not only simple, but may even be called barbaric. A nation like Norway has a great realistic drama without having ever had either a great classical drama or a great romantic drama. A nation like Russia makes us feel its modern fiction when we have never felt its ancient fiction. It has produced its Gissing without producing its Scott. Everything that is most sad and scientific, everything that is most grim and analytical, everything that can truly be called most modern, everything that can without unreasonableness be called most morbid, comes from these fresh and untried and unexhausted nationalities. Out of these infant peoples come the oldest voices of the earth.

This contradiction, like many other contradictions, is one which ought first of all to be registered as a mere fact; long before we attempt to explain why things contradict themselves, we ought, if we are honest men and good critics, to register the preliminary truth that things do contradict themselves. In this case, as I say, there are many possible and suggestive explanations. It may be, to take an example, that our modern Europe is so exhausted that even the vigorous expression of that exhaustion is difficult for every one except the most robust.

It may be that all the nations are tired; and it may be
that only the boldest and breeziest are not too tired to
say that they are tired. It may be that a man like Ibsen
in Norway or a man like Gorky in Russia are the only
people left who have so much faith that they can really
believe in scepticism. It may be that they are the only
people left who have so much animal spirits that they
can really feast high and drink deep at the ancient ban-
quet of pessimism. This is one of the possible hypo-
theses or explanations in the matter: that all Europe
feels these things and that they only have strength to
believe them also. Many other explanations might,
however, also be offered. It might be suggested that
half-barbaric countries, like Russia or Norway, which
have always lain, to say the least of it, on the extreme
edge of the circle of our European civilization, have a
certain primal melancholy which belongs to them
through all the ages. It is highly probable that this sadness, which to us is modern, is to them eternal. It is
highly probable that what we have solemnly and suddenly discovered in scientific text-books and philosophi-
cal magazines they absorbed and experienced thousands
of years ago, when they offered human sacrifice in black
and cruel forests and cried to their gods in the dark.
Their agnosticism is perhaps merely paganism; their
paganism, as in old times, is merely devil-worship. Certainly, Schopenhauer could hardly have written his hide-
ous essay on women except in a country which had once
been full of slavery and the service of fiends. It may
be that these moderns are tricking us altogether, and
are hiding in their current scientific jargon things that

they knew before science or civilization were. They
say that they are determinists; but the truth is, probably, that they are still worshipping the Norns. They
say that they describe scenes which are sickening and
dehumanizing in the name of art or in the name of
truth; but it may be that they do it in the name of
some deity indescribable, whom they propitiated with
blood and terror before the beginning of history.

This hypothesis, like the hypothesis mentioned before
it, is highly disputable, and is at best a suggestion. But
there is one broad truth in the matter which may in
any case be considered as established. A country like
Russia has far more inherent capacity for producing
revolution in revolutionists than any country of the type
of England or America. Communities highly civilized
and largely urban tend to a thing which is now called
evolution, the most cautious and the most conservative
of all social influences. The loyal Russian obeys the
Czar because he remembers the Czar and the Czar's importance. The disloyal Russian frets against the Czar
because he also remembers the Czar, and makes a note
of the necessity of knifing him. But the loyal English-
man obeys the upper classes because he has forgotten
that they are there. Their operation has become to him
like daylight, or gravitation, or any of the forces of nature. And there are no disloyal Englishmen; there are
no English revolutionists, because the oligarchic man-
agement of England is so complete as to be invisible.
The thing which can once get itself forgotten can make
itself omnipotent.

Gorky is preëminently Russian, in that he is a revolu-

tionist; not because most Russians are revolutionists
(for I imagine that they are not), but because most
Russians—indeed, nearly all Russians—are in that attitude of mind which makes revolution possible, and which
makes religion possible, an attitude of primary and dog-
matic assertion. To be a revolutionist it is first necessary to be a revelationist. It is necessary to believe in
the sufficiency of some theory of the universe or the
State. But in countries that have come under the influence of what is called the evolutionary idea, there has
been no dramatic righting of wrongs, and (unless the
evolutionary idea loses its hold) there never will be.
These countries have no revolution, they have to put
up with an inferior and largely fictitious thing which
they call progress.

The interest of the Gorky tale, like the interest of so
many other Russian masterpieces, consists in this sharp
contact between a simplicity, which we in the West feel
to be very old, and a rebelliousness which we in the
West feel to be very new. We cannot in our graduated
and polite civilization quite make head or tail of the
Russian anarch; we can only feel in a vague way that
his tale is the tale of the Missing Link, and that his
head is the head of the superman. We hear his lonely
cry of anger. But we cannot be quite certain whether
his protest is the protest of the first anarchist against
government, or whether it is the protest of the last savage against civilization. The cruelty of ages and of po-
litical cynicism or necessity has done much to burden
the race of which Gorky writes; but time has left them
one thing which it has not left to the people in Poplar

or West Ham. It has left them, apparently, the clear
and childlike power of seeing the cruelty which encom-
passes them. Gorky is a tramp, a man of the people,
and also a critic, and a bitter one. In the West poor
men, when they become articulate in literature, are
always sentimentalists and nearly always optimists.

It is no exaggeration to say that these people of whom
Gorky writes in such a story as "Creatures that once
were Men" are to the Western mind children. They
have, indeed, been tortured and broken by experience
and sin. But this has only sufficed to make them sad
children or naughty children or bewildered children.
They have absolutely no trace of that quality upon
which secure government rests so largely in Western
Europe, the quality of being soothed by long words as if
by an incantation. They do not call hunger "economic
pressure"; they call it hunger. They do not call rich
men "examples of capitalistic concentration," they call
them rich men. And this note of plainness and of something nobly prosaic is as characteristic of Gorky, in
some ways the most modern, and sophisticated of Russian authors, as it is of Tolstoy or any of the
Tolstoyan type of mind. The very title of this
story strikes the note of this sudden and simple
vision. The philanthropist writing long letters to the
Daily Telegraph says, of men living in a slum, that
"their degeneration is of such a kind as almost to pass
the limits of the semblance of humanity," and we read
the whole thing with a tepid assent as we should read
phrases about the virtues of Queen Victoria or the dig-
nity of the House of Commons. The Russian novelist,

when he describes a dosshouse, says, "Creatures that
once were Men." And we are arrested, and regard the
facts as a kind of terrible fairy tale. This story is a
test case of the Russian manner, for it is in itself a study
of decay, a study of failure, and a study of old age.
And yet the author is forced to write even of staleness
freshly; and though he is treating of the world as seen
by eyes darkened or blood-shot with evil experience, his
own eyes look out upon the scene with a clarity that is
almost babyish. Through all runs that curious Russian
sense that every man is only a man, which, if the Russians ever are a democracy, will make them the most
democratic democracy that the world has ever seen.
Take this passage, for instance, from the austere conclusion of "Creatures that once were Men":

Petunikoff smiled the smile of the conqueror and went
back into the dosshouse, but suddenly he stopped and trembled. At the door facing him stood an old man with a stick
in his hand and a large bag on his back, a horrible old man
in rags and tatters, which covered his bony figure. He bent
under the weight of his burden, and lowered his head on
his breast, as if he wished to attack the merchant.

"What are you? Who are you?" shouted Petunikoff.

"A man . . ." he answered, in a hoarse voice. This
hoarseness pleased and tranquillized Petunikoff, he even
smiled.

"A man! And are there really men like you?" Stepping
aside, he let the old man pass. He went, saying slowly:

"Men are of various kinds . . . as God wills . . . There
are worse than me . . . still worse . . . Yes . . ."

Here, in the very act of describing a kind of a fall

from humanity, Gorky expresses a sense of the strangeness and essential value of the human being which is far too commonly absent altogether from such complex civilizations as our own. To no Westerner, I am afraid, would it occur, when asked what he was, to say, "A man." He would be a plasterer who had walked from Reading, or an iron-puddler who had been thrown out of work in Lancashire, or a University man who would be really most grateful for the loan of five shillings, or the son of a lieutenant-general living in Brighton, who would not have made such an application if he had not known that he was talking to another gentleman. With us it is not a question of men being of various kinds; with us the kinds are almost different animals. But in spite of all Gorky's superficial scepticism and brutality, it is to him the fall from humanity, or the apparent fall from humanity, which is not merely great and lamentable, but essential and even mystical. The line between man and the beasts is one of the transcendental essentials of every religion; and it is, like most of the transcendental things of religion, identical with the main sentiments of the man of common sense. We feel this gulf when theologies say that it cannot be crossed. But we feel it quite as much (and that with a primal shudder) when philosophers or fanciful writers suggest that it might be crossed. And if any man wishes to discover whether or no he has really learned to regard the line between man and brute as merely relative and evolutionary, let him say again to himself those frightful words, "Creatures that once were Men."

G. K. CHESTERTON.

CREATURES THAT ONCE WERE MEN

CREATURES THAT ONCE WERE MEN

PART I

IN front of you is the main street, with two rows of miserable-looking huts with shuttered windows and old walls pressing on each other and leaning forward. The roofs of these time-worn habitations are full of holes, and have been patched here and there with laths; from underneath them project mildewed beams, which are shaded by the dusty-leaved elder-trees and crooked white willows—pitiable flora of those suburbs inhabited by the poor.

The dull green time-stained panes of the windows look upon each other with the cowardly glances of cheats. Through the street and toward the adjacent mountain runs the sinuous path, winding through the deep ditches filled with rain-water. Here and there are piled heaps of dust and other rubbish—either refuse or else put there purposely to keep the rain-water from flooding the houses. On the top of the mountain, among green gardens with dense foliage, beautiful stone houses lie hidden; the belfries of the churches rise proudly toward the sky, and their gilded crosses shine beneath the rays of the sun. During the rainy weather the neighboring town pours its water into this main road, which, at other times, is full of its dust, and all these

miserable houses seem, as it were, thrown by some powerful hand into that heap of dust, rubbish, and rain-
water.   They cling to the ground beneath the high
mountain, exposed to the sun, surrounded by decaying
refuse, and their sodden appearance impresses one with
the same feeling as would the half-rotten trunk of an
old tree.

At the end of the main street, as if thrown out of the
town, stood a two-storied house, which had been rented
from Petunikoff, a merchant and resident of the town.
It was in comparatively good order, being farther from
the mountain, while near it were the open fields, and
about half-a-mile away the river ran its winding course.

This large old house had the most dismal aspect amid
its surroundings.   The walls bent outward, and there
was hardly a pane of glass in any of the windows, except some of the fragments, which looked like the water
of the marshes—dull green.   The spaces of wall between
the windows were covered with spots, as if time were
trying to write there in hieroglyphics the history of the
old house, and the tottering roof added still more to its
pitiable condition.   It seemed as if the whole building
bent toward the ground, to await the last stroke of that
fate which should transform it into a chaos of rotting
remains, and finally into dust.

The gates were open, one-half of them displaced and
lying on the ground at the entrance, while between its
bars had grown the grass, which also covered the large
and empty court-yard.   In the depths of this yard stood
a low, iron-roofed, smoke-begrimed building.   The house
itself was of course unoccupied, but this shed, formerly

a blacksmith's forge, was now turned into a "doss-house," kept by a retired captain named Aristid Fomich Kuvalda.

In the interior of the dosshouse was a long, wide and grimy board, measuring some 28 by 70 feet. The room was lighted on one side by four small square windows, and on the other by a wide door. The unpainted brick walls were black with smoke, and the ceiling, which was built of timber, was almost black. In the middle stood a large stove, the furnace of which served as its founda-tion, and around this stove and along the walls were also long, wide boards, which served as beds for the lodgers. The walls smelt of smoke, the earthen floor of dampness, and the long, wide board of rotting rags.

The place of the proprietor was on the top of the stove, while the boards surrounding it were intended for those who were on good terms with the owner, and who were honored by his friendship. During the day the captain passed most of his time sitting on a kind of bench, made by himself by placing bricks against the wall of the court-yard, or else in the eating-house of Egor Vavilovitch, which was opposite the house, where he took all his meals and where he also drank vodki.

Before renting this house, Aristid Kuvalda had kept a registry office for servants in the town. If we look further back into his former life, we shall find that he once owned printing works, and previous to this, in his own words, he "just lived! And lived well too, Devil take it, and like one who knew how!"

He was a tall, broad-shouldered man of fifty, with a raw-looking face, swollen with drunkenness, and with a dirty yellowish beard. His eyes were large and gray, with an insolent expression of happiness. He spoke in a bass voice and with a sort of grumbling sound in his throat, and he almost always held between his teeth a German china pipe with a long bowl. When he was angry the nostrils of his big, crooked red nose swelled, and his lips trembled, exposing to view two rows of large and wolf-like yellow teeth. He had long arms, was lame, and always dressed in an old officer's uniform, with a dirty, greasy cap with a red band, a hat without a brim, and ragged felt boots which reached almost to his knees. In the morning, as a rule, he had a heavy drunken headache, and in the evening he caroused. However much he drank, he was never drunk, and so was always merry.

In the evenings he received lodgers, sitting on his brick-made bench with his pipe in his mouth.

"Whom have we here?" he would ask the ragged and tattered object approaching him, who had probably been chucked out of the town for drunkenness, or perhaps for some other reason not quite so simple. And after the man had answered him, he would say, "Let me see legal papers in confirmation of your lies." And if there were such papers they were shown. The captain would then put them in his bosom, seldom taking any interest in them, and would say:

"Everything is in order. Two kopecks for the night, ten kopecks for the week, and thirty kopecks for the month. Go and get a place for yourself, and see that it is not other people's, or else they will blow you up. The people that live here are particular."

"Don't you sell tea, bread, or anything to eat?"

"I trade only in walls and roofs, for which I pay to the swindling proprietor of this hole—Judas Petunikoff, merchant of the second guild—five roubles a month," explained Kuvalda in a business-like tone. "Only those come to me who are not accustomed to comfort and luxuries . . . . but if you are accustomed to eat every day, then there is the eating-house opposite. But it would be better for you if you left off that habit. You see you are not a gentleman. What do you eat? You eat yourself!"

For such speeches, delivered in a strictly business-like manner, and always with smiling eyes, and also for the attention he paid to his lodgers, the captain was very popular among the poor of the town. It very often happened that a former client of his would appear, not in rags, but in something more respectable and with a slightly happier face.

"Good-day, your honor, and how do you do?"

"Alive, in good health! Go on."

"Don't you know me?"

"I did not know you."

"Do you remember that I lived with you last winter for nearly a month . . . . when the fight with the police took place, and three were taken away?"

"My brother, that is so. The police do come even under my hospitable roof!"

"My God! You gave a piece of your mind to the police inspector of this district!"

"Wouldn't you accept some small hospitality from me? When I lived with you, you were . . ."

"Gratitude must be encouraged because it is seldom met with. You seem to be a good man, and, though I don't remember you, still I will go with you into the public-house and drink to your success and future prospects with the greatest pleasure."

"You seem always the same . . . . Are you always joking?"

"What else can one do, living among you unfortunate men?"

They went. Sometimes the Captain's former customer, uplifted and unsettled by the entertainment, returned to the dosshouse, and on the following morning they would again begin treating each other till the Captain's companion would wake up to realize that he had spent all his money in drink.

"Your honor, do you see that I have again fallen into your hands? What shall we do now?"

"The position, no doubt, is not a very good one, but still you need not trouble about it," reasoned the Captain. "You must, my friend, treat everything indifferently, without spoiling yourself by philosophy, and without asking yourself any question. To philosophize is always foolish; to philosophize with a drunken headache, ineffably so. Drunken headaches require vodki, and not the remorse of conscience or gnashing of teeth . . . save your teeth, or else you will not be able to protect yourself. Here are twenty kopecks. Go and buy a bottle of vodki for five kopecks, hot tripe or lungs, one pound of bread and two cucumbers. When we have lived off our drunken headache we will think of the condition of affairs . . ."

As a rule the consideration of the "condition of affairs" lasted some two or three days, and only when the Captain had not a farthing left of the three roubles or five roubles given him by his grateful customer did he say:

"You came! Do you see? Now that we have drunk everything with you, you fool, try again to regain the path of virtue and soberness. It has been truly said that if you do not sin, you will not repent, and, if you do not repent, you shall not be saved. We have done the first, and to repent is useless. Let us make direct for salvation. Go to the river and work, and if you think you cannot control yourself, tell the contractor, your employer, to keep your money, or else give it to me. When you get sufficient capital, I will get you a pair of trousers and other things necessary to make you seem a respectable and hard-working man, persecuted by fate. With decent-looking trousers you can go far. Now then, be off!"

Then the client would go to the river to work as a porter, smiling the while over the Captain's long and wise speeches. He did not distinctly understand them, but only saw in front of him two merry eyes, felt their encouraging influence, and knew that in the loquacious Captain he had an arm that would assist him in time of need.

And really it happened very often that, for a month or so, some ticket-of-leave client, under the strict surveillance of the Captain, had the opportunity of raising himself to a condition better than that to which, thanks to the Captain's coöperation, he had fallen.

"Now, then, my friend!" said the Captain, glancing critically at the restored client, "we have a coat and jacket. When I had respectable trousers I lived in town like a respectable man. But when the trousers wore out, I, too, fell off in the opinion of my fellow-men and had to come down here from the town. Men, my fine mannikin, judge everything by the outward appearance, while, owing to their foolishness, the actual reality of things is incomprehensible to them. Make a note of this on your nose, and pay me at least half your debt. Go in peace; seek, and you may find."

"How much do I owe you, Aristid Fomich?" asks the client, in confusion.

"One rouble and 70 kopecks. . . . Now, give me only one rouble, or, if you like, 70 kopecks, and as for the rest, I shall wait until you have earned more than you have now by stealing or by hard work, it does not matter to me."

"I thank you humbly for your kindness!" says the client, touched to the heart. "Truly you are a kind man. . . . . ; Life has persecuted you in vain. . . . What an eagle you would have been in your own place!"

The Captain could not live without eloquent speeches.

"What does 'in my own place' mean? No one really knows his own place in life, and every one of us crawls into his harness. The place of the merchant Judas Petunikoff ought to be in penal servitude, but he still walks through the streets in daylight, and even intends to build a factory. The place of our teacher ought to be beside a wife and half-a-dozen children, but he is loitering in the public-house of Vaviloff. And then, there is yourself. You are going to seek a situation as a hall porter or waiter, but I can see that you ought to be a soldier in the army, because you are no fool, are patient and understand discipline. Life shuffles us like cards, you see, and it is only accidentally, and only for a time, that we fall into our own places!"

Such farewell speeches often served as a preface to the continuation of their acquaintance, which again began with drinking and went so far that the client would spend his last farthing. Then the Captain would stand him treat, and they would drink all they had.

A repetition of similar doings did not affect in the least the good relations of the parties.

The teacher mentioned by the Captain was another of those customers who were thus reformed only in order that they should sin again. Thanks to his intellect, he was the nearest in rank to the Captain, and this was probably the cause of his falling so low as dosshouse life, and of his inability to rise again. It was only with him that Aristid Kuvalda could philosophize with the certainty of being understood. He valued this, and when the reformed teacher prepared to leave the dosshouse in order to get a corner in town for himself, then Aristid Kuvalda accompanied him so sorrowfully and sadly that it ended, as a rule, in their both getting drunk and spending all their money. Probably Kuvalda arranged the matter intentionally so that the teacher could not leave the dosshouse, though he desired to do so with all his heart. Was it possible for Aristid Kuvalda, a nobleman (as was evident from his speeches), one who was accustomed to think, though the turn of fate may have changed his position, was it possible for him not to desire to have close to him a man like himself? We can pity our own faults in others.

This teacher had once taught at an institution in one of the towns on the Volga, but in consequence of some story was dismissed. After this he was a clerk in a tannery, but again had to leave. Then he became a librarian in some private library, subsequently following other professions. Finally, after passing examinations in law he became a lawyer, but drink reduced him to the Captain's dosshouse. He was tall, round-shouldered, with a long, sharp nose and bald head. In his bony and yellow face, on which grew a wedge-shaped beard, shone large, restless eyes, deeply sunk in their sockets, and the corners of his mouth drooped sadly down. He earned his bread, or rather his drink, by reporting for the local papers. He sometimes earned as much as fifteen roubles. These he gave to the Captain and said:

"It is enough. I am going back into the bosom of culture. Another week's hard work and I shall dress respectably, and then *Addio, mio caro!*"

"Very exemplary! As I heartily sympathize with your decision, Philip, I shall not give you another glass all this week," the Captain warned him sternly.

"I shall be thankful! . . . . You will not give me one drop?"

The Captain heard in his voice a beseeching note to which he turned a deaf ear.

"Even though you roar, I shall not give it you!"

"As you like, then," sighed the teacher, and went away to continue his reporting. But after a day or two he would return tired and thirsty, and would look at the Captain with a beseeching glance out of the corners of his eyes, hoping that his friend's heart would soften.

The Captain in such cases put on a serious face and began speaking with killing irony on the theme of weakness of character, of the animal delight of intoxication, and on such subjects as suited the occasion. One must do him justice: he was captivated by his *rôle* of mentor and moralist, but the lodgers dogged him, and, listening sceptically to his exhortations to repentance, would whisper aside to each other:

"Cunning, skilful, shifty rogue! I told you so, but you would not listen. It's your own fault!"

"His honor is really a good soldier. He goes first and examines the road behind him!"

The teacher then hunted here and there till he found his friend again in some corner, and grasping his dirty coat, trembling and licking his dry lips, looked into his face with a deep, tragic glance, without articulate words.

"Can't you?" asked the Captain sullenly.

The teacher answered by bowing his head and letting it fall on his breast, his tall, thin body trembling the while.

"Wait another day . . . perhaps you will be all right then," proposed Kuvalda. The teacher sighed, and shook his head hopelessly.

The Captain saw that his friend's thin body trembled with the thirst for the poison, and took some money from his pocket.

"In the majority of cases it is impossible to fight against fate," said he, as if trying to justify himself

before someone. But if the teacher controlled himself
for a whole week, then there was a touching farewell
scene between the two friends, which ended as a rule
in the eating-house of Vaviloff. The teacher did not
spend all his money, but spent at least half on the children of the main street. The poor are always rich in
children, and in the dirt and ditches of this street there
were groups of them from morning to night, hungry,
naked and dirty. Children are the living flowers of the
earth, but these had the appearance of flowers that have
faded prematurely, because they grew in ground where
there was no healthy nourishment. Often the teacher
would gather them round him, would buy them bread,
eggs, apples and nuts, and take them into the fields by
the river side. There they would sit and greedily eat
everything he offered them, after which they would
begin to play, filling the fields for a mile around with
careless noise and laughter. The tall, thin figure of the
drunkard towered above these small people, who treated
him familiarly, as if he were one of their own age. They
called him "Philip," and did not trouble to prefix
"Uncle" to his name. Playing around him, like little
wild animals, they pushed him, jumped upon his back,
beat him upon his bald head, and caught hold of his
nose. All this must have pleased him, as he did not
protest against such liberties. He spoke very little to
them, and when he did so he did it cautiously as if
afraid that his words would hurt or contaminate them.
He passed many hours thus as their companion and
plaything, watching their lively faces with his gloomy
eyes. Then he would thoughtfully and slowly direct his

steps to the eating-house of Vaviloff, where he would drink silently and quickly till all his senses left him.

*   *   *   *   *

Almost every day after his reporting he would bring a newspaper, and then gather round him all these creatures that once were men. On seeing him, they would come forward from all corners of the court-yard, drunk, or suffering from drunken headache, dishevelled, tattered, miserable, and pitiable. Then would come the barrel-like, stout Aleksei Maksimovitch Simtsoff, formerly Inspector of Woods and Forests, under the Department of Appendages, but now trading in matches, ink, blacking, and lemons. He was an old man of sixty, in a canvas overcoat and a wide-brimmed hat, the greasy borders of which hid his stout, fat, red face. He had a thick white beard, out of which a small red nose turned gaily heavenward. He had thick, crimson lips and watery, cynical eyes. They called him "Kubar," a name which well described his round figure and buzzing speech. After him, Kanets appeared from some corner—a dark, sad-looking, silent drunkard: then the former governor of the prison, Luka Antonovitch Martyanoff, a man who existed on "remeshok," "trilistika," and "bankovka," * and many such cunning games, not much appreciated by the police. He would throw his

---

Note by translator.—Well-known games of chance, played by the lower classes. The police specially endeavor to stop them, but unsuccessfully.

hard and oft-scourged body on the grass beside the teacher, and, turning his eyes round and scratching his head, would ask in a hoarse, bass voice, "May I?"

Then appeared Pavel Solntseff, a man of thirty years of age, suffering from consumption. The ribs of his left side had been broken in a quarrel, and the sharp, yellow face, like that of a fox, always wore a malicious smile. The thin lips, when opened, exposed two rows of decayed black teeth, and the rags on his shoulders swayed backward and forward as if they were hung on a clothespole. They called him "Abyedok." He hawked brushes and bath brooms of his own manufacture, good, strong brushes made from a peculiar kind of grass.

Then followed a lean and bony man of whom no one knew anything, with a frightened expression in his eyes, the left one of which had a squint. He was silent and timid, and had been imprisoned three times for theft by the High Court of Justice and the Magisterial Courts. His family name was Kiselnikoff, but they called him Paltara Taras, because he was a head and shoulders taller than his friend, Deacon Taras, who had been degraded from his office for drunkenness and immorality. The Deacon was a short, thick-set person, with the chest of an athlete and a round, strong head. He danced skilfully, and was still more skilful at swearing. He and Paltara Taras worked in the wood on the banks of the river, and in free hours he told his friend or any one who would listen, "Tales of my own composition," as he used to say. On hearing these stories, the heroes of which always seemed to be saints, kings, priests, or generals, even the inmates of the dosshouse spat and rubbed their eyes in astonishment at the imagination of the Deacon, who told them shameless tales of lewd, fantastic adventures, with blinking eyes and a passionless expression of countenance. The imagination of this man was powerful and inexhaustible; he could go on relating and composing all day, from morning to night, without once repeating what he had said before. In his expression you sometimes saw the poet gone astray, sometimes the romancer, and he always succeeded in making his tales realistic by the effective and powerful words in which he told them.

There was also a foolish young man called Kuvalda Meteor. One night he came to sleep in the dosshouse, and had remained ever since among these men, much to their astonishment. At first they did not take much notice of him. In the daytime, like all the others, he went away to find something to eat, but at nights he always loitered around this friendly company till at last the Captain took notice of him.

"Boy! What business have you here on this earth?"

The boy answered boldly and stoutly:

"I am a barefooted tramp . . . ."

The Captain looked critically at him. This youngster had long hair and a weak face, with prominent cheekbones and a turned-up nose. He was dressed in a blue blouse without a waistband, and on his head he wore the remains of a straw hat, while his feet were bare.

"You are a fool!" decided Aristid Kuvalda. "What are you knocking about here for? You are of absolutely no use to us . . . Do you drink vodki? . . . No? . . . Well, then, can you steal?" Again, "No." "Go away, learn, and come back again when you know something, and are a man . . ."

The youngster smiled.

"No. I shall live with you."

"Why?"

"Just because . . ."

"Oh, you . . . Meteor!" said the Captain.

"I will break his teeth for him," said Martyanoff.

"And why?" asked the youngster.

"Just because. . . ."

"And I will take a stone and hit you on the head," the young man answered respectfully.

Martyanoff would have broken his bones, had not Kuvalda interrupted with:

"Leave him alone. . . . Is this a home to you or even to us? You have no sufficient reason to break his teeth for him. You have no better reason than he for living with us."

"Well, then, Devil take him! . . . We all live in the world without sufficient reason. . . . We live, and why? Because! He also because . . . let him alone. . . ."

"But it is better for you, young man, to go away from us," the teacher advised him, looking him up and down with his sad eyes. He made no answer, but remained. And they soon became accustomed to his presence, and ceased to take any notice of him. But he lived among them, and observed everything.

The above were the chief members of the Captain's company, and he called them with kind-hearted sarcasm "Creatures that once were Men." For though there were men who had experienced as much of the bitter irony of fate as these men, yet they were not fallen so low. Not infrequently, respectable men belonging to the cultured classes are inferior to those belonging to the peasantry, and it is always a fact that the depraved man from the city is immeasurably worse than the depraved man from the village. This fact was strikingly illustrated by the contrast between the formerly well-educated men and the mujiks who were living in Kuvalda's shelter.

The representative of the latter class was an old mujik called Tyapa. Tall and angular, he kept his head in such a position that his chin touched his breast. He was the Captain's first lodger, and it was said of him that he had a great deal of money hidden somewhere, and for its sake had nearly had his throat cut some two years ago: ever since then he carried his head thus. Over his eyes hung grayish eyebrows, and, looked at in profile, only his crooked nose was to be seen. His shadow reminded one of a poker. He denied that he had money, and said that they "only tried to cut his throat out of malice," and from that day he took to collecting rags, and that is why his head was always bent as if incessantly looking on the ground. When he went about shaking his head, and minus a walking-stick in his hand, and a bag on his back—the signs of his profession—he seemed to be thinking almost to madness, and, at such times, Kuvalda spoke thus, pointing to him with his finger:

"Look, there is the conscience of Merchant Judas Petunikoff. See how disorderly, dirty, and low is the escaped conscience."

Tyapa, as a rule, spoke in a hoarse and hardly audible voice, and that is why he spoke very little, and loved to be alone. But whenever a stranger, compelled to leave the village, appeared in the dosshouse, Tyapa seemed sadder and angrier, and followed the unfortunate about with biting jeers and a wicked chuckling in his throat. He either put some beggar against him, or himself threatened to rob and beat him, till the frightened mujik would disappear from the dosshouse and never more be seen. Then Tyapa was quiet again, and would sit in some corner mending his rags, or else reading his Bible, which was as dirty, worn, and old as himself. Only when the teacher brought a newspaper and began reading did he come from his corner once more. As a rule, Tyapa listened to what was read silently and sighed often, without asking anything of anyone. But once when the teacher, having read the paper, wanted to put it away, Tyapa stretched out his bony hand, and said, "Give it to me . . ."

"What do you want it for?"

"Give it to me . . . Perhaps there is something in it about us . . ."

"About whom?"

"About the village."

They laughed at him, and threw him the paper. He took it, and read in it how in the village the hail had destroyed the cornfields, how in another village fire destroyed thirty houses, and that in a third a woman had poisoned her family—in fact, everything that it is customary to write of—everything, that is to say, which is bad, and which depicts only the worst side of the unfortunate village. Tyapa read all this silently and roared, perhaps from sympathy, perhaps from delight at the sad news.

He passed the whole Sunday in reading his Bible, and never went out collecting rags on that day. While reading, he groaned and sighed continually. He kept the book close to his breast, and was angry with any one who interrupted him or who touched his Bible.

"Oh, you drunken blackguard," said Kuvalda to him, "what do you understand of it?"

"Nothing, wizard! I don't understand anything, and I do not read any books . . . But I read . . ."

"Therefore you are a fool . . ." said the Captain, decidedly. "When there are insects in your head, you know it is uncomfortable, but if some thoughts enter there too, how will you live then, you old toad?"

"I have not long to live," said Tyapa, quietly.

Once the teacher asked how he had learned to read.

"In prison," answered Tyapa shortly.

"Have you been there?"

"I was there. . . ."

"For what?"

"Just so. . . . It was a mistake. . . . But I brought the Bible out with me from there. A lady gave it to me. . . . It is good in prison, brother."

"Is that so? And why?"

"It teaches one. . . . I learned to read there. . . . I also got this book. . . . And all these you see, free. . . ."

When the teacher appeared in the dosshouse, Tyapa had already lived there for some time. He looked long into the teacher's face, as if to discover what kind of a man he was.

Tyapa often listened to his conversation, and once, sitting down beside him, said:

"I see you are very learned. . . . Have you read the Bible?"

"I have read it. . . ."

"I see; I see. . . . Can you remember it?"

"Yes. . . . I remember it. . . ."

Then the old man leaned to one side and gazed at the other with a serious, suspicious glance.

"There were the Amalekites, do you remember?"

"Well?"

"Where are they now?"

"Disappeared . . . Tyapa . . . died out . . ."

The old man was silent, then asked again: "And where are the Philistines?"

"These also . . ."

"Have all these died out?"

"Yes . . . all . . ."

"And so . . . we also will die out?"

"There will come a time when we also will die," said the teacher indifferently.

"And to what tribe of Israel do we belong?"

The teacher looked at him, and began telling him about Scythians and Slavs. . . .

The old man became all the more frightened, and glanced at his face.

"You are lying!" he said scornfully, when the teacher had finished.

"What lie have I told?" asked the teacher.

"You mentioned tribes that are not mentioned in the Bible."

He got up and walked away, angry and deeply insulted.

"You will go mad, Tyapa," called the teacher after him with conviction.

Then the old man came back again, and stretching out his hand, threatened him with his crooked and dirty finger.

"God made Adam—from Adam were descended the Jews, that means that all people are descended from Jews . . . and we also . . ."

"Well?"

"Tartars are descended from Ishmael, but he also came of the Jews . . ."

"What do you want to tell me all this for?"

"Nothing! Only why do you tell lies?" Then he walked away, leaving his companion in perplexity. But after two days he came again and sat by him.

"You are learned . . . Tell me, then, whose descendants are we? Are we Babylonians, or who are we?"

"We are Slavs, Tyapa," said the teacher, and attentively awaited his answer, wishing to understand him.

"Speak to me from the Bible. There are no such men there."

Then the teacher began criticizing the Bible. The old man listened, and interrupted him after a long while.

"Stop . . . Wait! That means that among people known to God there are no Russians? We are not known to God? Is it so? God knew all those who are mentioned in the Bible . . . . He destroyed them by sword and fire, He destroyed their cities; but He also sent prophets to teach them. That means that He also pitied them. He scattered the Jews and the Tartars . . . But what about us? Why have we prophets no longer?"

"Well, I don't know!" replied the teacher, trying to understand the old man. But the latter put his hand on the teacher's shoulder, and slowly pushed him backward and forward, and his throat made a noise as if he were swallowing something. . . . .

"Tell me! You speak so much . . . as if you knew everything. It makes me sick to listen to you . . . you darken my soul. . . . I should be better pleased if you were silent. Who are we, eh? Why have we no prophets? Ha, ha! . . . Where were we when Christ walked on this earth? Do you see? And you too, you are lying. . . . Do you think that all die out? The Russian people will never disappear. . . . You are lying. . . . It has been written in the Bible, only it is not known what name the Russians are given. Do you see what kind of people they are? They are numberless. . . . How many villages are there on the earth? Think of all the people who live on it, so strong, so numerous! And you say that they will die out; men shall die, but God wants the people, God the Creator of the earth! The Amalekites did not die out. They are either German or French. . . . But you, eh, you! Now then, tell me why we are abandoned by God? Have we no punishments nor prophets from the Lord? Who then will teach us?" Tyapa spoke strongly and plainly, and

there was faith in his words. He had been speaking a
long time, and the teacher, who was generally drunk
and in a speechless condition, could not stand it any
longer. He looked at the dry, wrinkled old man, felt
the great force of these words, and suddenly began to
pity himself. He wished to say something so strong
and convincing to the old man that Tyapa would be
disposed in his favor; he did not wish to speak in such
a serious, earnest way, but in a soft and fatherly tone.
And the teacher felt as if something were rising from
his breast into his throat . . . But he could not find
any powerful words.

"What kind of a man are you? . . . Your soul seems
to be torn away—and you still continue speaking . . .
as if you knew something . . . It would be better if
you were silent."

"Ah, Tyapa, what you say is true," replied the teacher
sadly. "The people . . . you are right . . . they are
numberless . . . but I am a stranger to them . . . and
they are strangers to me . . . Do you see where the
tragedy of my life is hidden? . . . But let me alone!
I shall suffer . . . and there are no prophets also . . .
No. You are right, I speak a great deal . . . But it is
no good to anyone. I shall be always silent . . . Only
don't speak with me like this . . . Ah, old man, you do
not know . . . You do not know . . . And you cannot
understand."

And in the end the teacher cried. He cried so easily
and so freely, with such torrents of flowing tears, that
he soon found relief.

"You ought to go into a village . . . become a clerk

or a teacher . . . You would be well fed there. What are you crying for?" asked Tyapa sadly.

But the teacher was crying as if the tears quieted and comforted him.

From this day they became friends, and the "creatures that once were men," seeing them together, said: "The teacher is friendly with Tyapa . . . He wishes his money. Kuvalda must have put this into his head . . . To look about to see where the old man's fortune is . . ."

Probably they did not believe what they said. There was one strange thing about these men, namely, that they painted themselves to others worse than they actually were. A man who has good in him does not mind sometimes showing his worse nature.

*　　*　　*　　*　　*

When all these people were gathered round the teacher, then the reading of the newspaper would begin.

"Well, what does the newspaper discuss to-day? Is there any feuilleton?"

"No," the teacher informs him.

"Your publisher seems greedy . . . but is there any leader?"

"There is one to-day. . . . It appears to be by Gul-yaeff."

"Aha! Come, out with it! He writes cleverly, the rascal."

" 'The taxation of immovable property,' " reads the teacher, " 'was introduced some fifteen years ago, and up to the present it has served as the basis for collecting these taxes in aid of the city revenue . . .' "

"That is simple," comments Captain Kuvalda. "It continues to serve. That is ridiculous. To the merchant who is moving about in the city, it is profitable that it should continue to serve. Therefore it does continue."

"The article, in fact, is written on the subject," says the teacher.

"Is it? That is strange, it is more a subject for a feuilleton . . ."

"Such a subject must be treated with plenty of pepper. . . ."

Then a short discussion begins. The people listen attentively, as only one bottle of vodki has been drunk.

After the leader, they read the local events, then the court proceedings, and, if in the police court it reports that the defendant or plaintiff is a merchant, then Aristid Kuvalda sincerely rejoices. If someone has robbed the merchant, "That is good," says he. "Only it is a pity they robbed him of so little." If his horses have broken down, "It is sad that he is still alive." If the merchant has lost his suit in court, "It is a pity that the costs were not double the amount."

"That would have been illegal," remarks the teacher.

"Illegal! But is the merchant himself legal?" inquires Kuvalda bitterly. "What is the merchant? Let us investigate this rough and uncouth phenomenon. First of all, every merchant is a mujik. He comes from a village, and in course of time becomes a merchant. In order to be a merchant, one must have money. Where can the mujik get the money from? It is well known that he does not get it by honest hard work, and that means that the mujik, somehow or other, has been swindling. That is to say, a merchant is simply a dishonest mujik."

"Splendid!" cry the people, approving the orator's deduction, and Tyapa bellows all the time, scratching his breast. He always bellows like this as he drinks his first glass of vodki, when he has a drunken headache. The Captain beams with joy. They next read the correspondence. This is, for the Captain, "an abundance of drinks," as he himself calls it. He always notices how the merchants make this life abominable, and how cleverly they spoil everything. His speeches thunder at and annihilate merchants. His audience listens to him with the greatest pleasure, because he swears atrociously. "If I wrote for the papers," he shouts, "I would show up the merchant in his true colors . . . I would show that he is a beast, playing for a time the *rôle* of a man. I understand him! He is a rough boor, does not know the meaning of the words 'good taste,' has no notion of patriotism, and his knowledge is not worth five kopecks."

Abyedok, knowing the Captain's weak point, and fond of making other people angry, cunningly adds:

"Yes, since the nobility began to make acquaintance with hunger, men have disappeared from the world . . ."

"You are right, you son of a spider and a toad. Yes, from the time that the noblemen fell, there have been no men. There are only merchants, and I hate them."

"That is easy to understand, brother, because you too, have been brought down by them . . ."

"I? I was ruined by love of life . . . Fool that I was, I loved life, but the merchant spoils it, and I cannot bear it, simply for this reason, and not because I am a nobleman. But if you want to know the truth, I was once a man, though I was not noble. I care now for nothing and nobody . . . and all my life has been tame—a sweetheart who has jilted me—therefore I despise life, and am indifferent to it."

"You lie!" says Abyedok.

"I lie?" roars Aristid Kuvalda, almost crimson with anger.

"Why shout?" comes in the cold. sad voice of Martyanoff.

"Why judge others? Merchants, noblemen . . . what have we to do with them?"

"Seeing that we are" . . . puts in Deacon Taras.

"Be quiet, Abyedok," says the teacher good-naturedly. "Why do you provoke him?" He does not love either discussion or noise, and when they quarrel all around him his lips form into a sickly grimace, and he endeavors quietly and reasonably to reconcile each with the other, and if he does not succeed in this he leaves the company. Knowing this, the Captain, if he is not very drunk, controls himself, not wishing to lose, in the person of the teacher, one of the best of his listeners.

"I repeat," he continues, in a quieter tone, "that I see life in the hands of enemies, not only enemies of the noble but of everything good, avaricious and incapable of adorning existence in any way."

"But all the same," says the teacher, "merchants, so to speak, created Genoa, Venice, Holland—and all these were merchants, merchants from England, India, the Stroyanoff merchants . . ."

"I do not speak of these men, I am thinking of Judas Petunikoff, who is one of them. . . ."

"And you say you have nothing to do with them?" asks the teacher quietly.

"But do you think that I do not live? Aha! I do live, but I suppose I ought not to be angry at the fact that life is desecrated and robbed of all freedom by these men."

"And they dare to laugh at the kindly anger of the Captain, a man living in retirement?" says Abyedok teasingly.

"Very well! I agree with you that I am foolish. Being a creature who was once a man, I ought to blot out from my heart all those feelings that once were mine. You may be right, but then how could I or any of you defend ourselves if we did away with all these feelings?"

"Now then, you are talking sense," says the teacher encouragingly.

"We want other feelings and other views on life. . . . We want something new . . . because we ourselves are a novelty in this life. . . ."

"Doubtless this is most important for us," remarks the teacher.

"Why?" asks Kanets. "Is it not all the same whatever we say or think? We have not got long to live . . . I am forty, you are fifty . . . there is no one among us younger than thirty, and even at twenty one cannot live such a life long."

"And what kind of novelty are we?" asked Abyedok mockingly.

"Since nakedness has always existed . . ."

"Yes, and it created Rome," said the teacher.

"Yes, of course," says the Captain, beaming with joy. "Romulus and Remus, ·eh? We also shall create when our time comes . . ."

"Violation of public peace," interrupts Abyedok. He laughs in a self-satisfied way. His laughter is impudent and insolent, and is echoed by Simtsoff, the Deacon and Paltara Taras. The naïve eyes of young Meteor light up, and his cheeks flush crimson.

Kanets speaks, and it seems as if he were hammering their heads.

"All these are foolish illusions . . . fiddlesticks!"

It was strange to see them reasoning in this manner, these outcasts from life, tattered, drunken with vodki and wickedness, filthy and forlorn. Such conversations rejoiced the Captain's heart. They gave him an opportunity of speaking more, and therefore he thought himself better than the rest. However low he may fall, a man can never deny himself the delight of feeling cleverer, more powerful, or even better fed than his companions. Aristid Kuvalda abused this pleasure, and never could have enough of it, much to the disgust of Abyedok, Kubar, and others of these creatures that once were men, who were less interested in such things.

Politics, however, were more to the popular taste. The discussions as to the necessity of taking India or of subduing England were lengthy and protracted. Nor did they speak with less enthusiasm of the radical measure of clearing Jews off the face of the earth. On this subject Abyedok was always the first to propose dreadful plans to effect the desired end, but the Captain, always first in every other argument, did not join in this one. They also spoke much and impudently about women, but the teacher always defended them, and sometimes was very angry when they went so far as to pass the limits of decency. They all, as a rule, gave in to him, because they did not look upon him as a common person, and also because they wished to borrow from him on Saturdays the money which he had earned during the week. He had many privileges. They never beat him, for instance, on these occasions when the conversation ended in a free fight. He had the right to bring women into the dosshouse; a privilege accorded to no one else, as the Captain had previously warned them.

"No bringing of women to my house," he had said. "Women, merchants and philosophers, these are the three causes of my ruin. I will horsewhip anyone bringing in women. I will horsewhip the woman also. . . . And as to the philosopher, I'll knock his head off for him." And notwithstanding his age he could have knocked anyone's head off, for he possessed wonderful strength. Besides that, whenever he fought or quarrelled, he was assisted by Martyanoff, who was accustomed during a general fight to stand silently and sadly back to back with Kuvalda, when he became an all-destroying and impregnable engine of war. Once when Simtsoff was drunk, he rushed at the teacher for no

reason whatever, and getting hold of his head tore out
a bunch of hair. Kuvalda, with one stroke of his fist
in the other's chest, sent him spinning, and he fell to
the ground. He was unconscious for almost half-an-
hour, and when he came to himself Kuvalda compelled
him to eat the hair he had torn from the teacher's head.
He ate it, preferring this to being beaten to death.

Besides reading newspapers, fighting and indulging in
general conversation, they amused themselves by playing
cards. They played without Martyanoff because he could
not play honestly. After cheating several times, he
openly confessed:

"I cannot play without cheating . . . it is a habit of
mine."

"Habits do get the better of you," assented Deacon
Taras. "I always used to beat my wife every Sunday
after Mass, and when she died I cannot describe how
extremely dull I felt every Sunday. I lived through
one Sunday—it was dreadful, the second I still controlled myself, the third Sunday I struck my Asok.
. . . She was angry and threatened to summon me.
Just imagine if she had done so! On the fourth Sunday, I beat her just as if she were my own wife! After
that I gave her ten roubles, and beat her according to
my own rules till I married again!" . . .

"You are lying, Deacon! How could you marry a
second time?" interrupted Abyedok.

"Ay, just so . . . She looked after my house. . . ."

"Did you have any children?" asked the teacher.

"Five of them. . . . One was drowned . . . the
oldest . . . he was an amusing boy! Two died of diph-

theria . . . One of the daughters married a student and went with him to Siberia. The other went to the University of St. Petersburg and died there . . . of consumption they say. Ye—es, there were five of them. . . . Ecclesiastics are prolific, you know." He began explaining why this was so, and they laughed till they nearly burst at his tales. When the laughter stopped, Aleksei Maksimovitch Simtsoff remembered that he too had once had a daughter.

"Her name was Lidka . . . she was very stout . . ." More than this he did not seem to remember, for he looked at them all, was silent and smiled . . . in a guilty way. Those men spoke very little to each other about their past, and they recalled it very seldom, and then only its general outlines. When they did mention it, it was in a cynical tone. Probably, this was just as well, since, in many people, remembrance of the past kills all present energy and deadens all hope for the future.

*   *   *   *   *

On rainy, cold, or dull days in the late autumn, these "creatures that once were men" gathered in the eating-house of Vaviloff. They were well known there, where some feared them as thieves and rogues, and some looked upon them contemptuously as hard drinkers, although they respected them, thinking that they were clever.

The eating-house of Vaviloff was the club of the main street, and the "creatures that once were men" were its most intellectual members. On Saturday evenings or

Sunday mornings, when the eating-house was packed, the "creatures that once were men" were only too welcome guests. They brought with them, besides the forgotten and poverty-stricken inhabitants of the street, their own spirit, in which there was something that brightened the lives of men exhausted and worn out in the struggle for existence, as great drunkards as the inhabitants of Kuvalda's shelter, and, like them, outcasts from the town. Their ability to speak on all subjects, their freedom of opinion, skill in repartee, courage in the presence of those of whom the whole street was in terror, together with their daring demeanor, could not but be pleasing to their companions. Then, too, they were well versed in law, and could advise, write petitions, and help to swindle without incurring the risk of punishment. For all this they were paid with vodki and flattering admiration of their talents.

The inhabitants of the street were divided into two parties according to their sympathies. One was in favor of Kuvalda, who was thought "a good soldier, clever, and courageous"; the other was convinced of the fact that the teacher was "superior" to Kuvalda. The latter's admirers were those who were known to be drunkards, thieves, and murderers, for whom the road from beggary to prison was inevitable. But those who respected the teacher were men who still had expectations, still hoped for better things, who were eternally occupied with nothing, and who were nearly always hungry.

The nature of the teacher's and Kuvalda's relations toward the street may be gathered from the following:

Once in the eating-house they were discussing the resolution passed by the Corporation regarding the main street, viz., that the inhabitants were to fill up the pits and ditches in the street, and that neither manure nor the dead bodies of domestic animals should be used for the purpose, but only broken tiles, etc., from the ruins of other houses.

"Where am I going to get these same broken tiles and bricks? I could not get sufficient bricks together to build a hen-house," plaintively said Mokei Anisimoff, a man who hawked kalaches (a sort of white bread) which were baked by his wife.

"Where can you get broken bricks and lime rubbish? Take bags with you, and go and remove them from the Corporation buildings. They are so old that they are of no use to anyone, and you will thus be doing two good deeds; firstly, by repairing the main street; and secondly, by adorning the city with a new Corporation building."

"If you want horses, get them from the Lord Mayor, and take his three daughters, who seem quite fit for harness. Then destroy the house of Judas Petunikoff and pave the street with its timbers. By the way, Mokei, I know out of what your wife baked to-day's kalaches; out of the frames of the third window and the two steps from the roof of Judas' house."

When those present had laughed and joked sufficiently over the Captain's proposal, the sober market gardener, Pavlyugus asked:

"But seriously, what are we to do, your honor? . . . Eh? What do you think?"

"I? I shall neither move hand nor foot. If they wish to clean the street, let them do it."

"Some of the houses are almost coming down. . . ."

"Let them fall; don't interfere; and when they fall ask help from the city. If they don't give it you, then bring a suit in court against them! Where does the water come from? From the city! Therefore let the city be responsible for the destruction of the houses."

"They will say it is rain-water."

"Does it destroy the houses in the city? Eh? They take taxes from you, but they do not permit you to speak! They destroy your property and at the same time compel you to repair it!" And half the radicals in the street, convinced by the words of Kuvalda, decided to wait till the rain-water came down in huge streams and swept away their houses. The others, more sensible, found in the teacher a man who composed for them an excellent and convincing report for the Corporation. In this report the refusal of the street's inhabitants to comply with the resolution of the Corporation was so well explained that the Corporation actually entertained it. It was decided that the rubbish left after some repairs had been done to the barracks should be used for mending and filling up the ditches in their street, and for the transport of this five horses were given by the fire brigade. Still more, they even saw the necessity of laying a drain-pipe through the street. This and many other things vastly increased the popularity of the teacher. He wrote petitions for them and published various remarks in the newspapers. For 'nstance, on one occasion Vaviloff's customers noticed that the herrings and other provisions of the eating-house were not what they should be, and after a day or two they saw Vaviloff standing at the bar with the newspaper in his hand making a public apology.

"It is true, I must acknowledge, that I bought old and not very good herrings, and the cabbage . . . also . . . was old. It is only too well known that anyone can put many a five-kopeck piece in his pocket in this way. And what is the result? It has not been a success; I was greedy, I own, but the cleverer man has exposed me, so we are quits . . ."

This confession made a very good impression on the people, and it also gave Vaviloff the opportunity of still feeding them with herrings and cabbages which were not good, though they failed to notice it, so much were they impressed.

This incident was very significant, because it increased not only the teacher's popularity, but also the effect of press opinion.

It often happened, too, that the teacher read lectures on practical morality in the eating-house.

"I saw you," he said to the painter, Yashka Tyarin; "I saw you, Yakov, beating your wife . . ."

Yashka was "touched with paint" after having two glasses of vodki, and was in a slightly uplifted condition.

The people looked at him, expecting him to make a row, and all were silent.

"Did you see me? And how did it please you?" asks Yashka.

The people control their laughter.

"No; it did not please me," replies the teacher. His tone is so serious that the people are silent.

"You see I was just trying it," said Yashka, with bravado, fearing that the teacher would rebuke him. "The wife is satisfied. . . . She has not got up yet to-day. . . ."

The teacher, who was drawing absently with his fingers on the table, said, "Do you see, Yakov, why this did not please me? . . . Let us go into the matter thoroughly, and understand what you are really doing, and what the result may be. Your wife is pregnant. You struck her last night on her sides and breast. That means that you beat not only her but the child too. You may have killed him, and your wife might have died or else have become seriously ill. To have the trouble of looking after a sick woman is not pleasant. It is wearing, and would cost you dear, because illness requires medicine, and medicine money. If you have not killed the child, you may have crippled him, and he will be born deformed, lop-sided, or hunch-backed. That means that he will not be able to work, and it is only too important to you that he should be a good workman. Even if he be born ill, it will be bad enough, because he will keep his mother from work, and will require medicine. Do you see what you are doing to yourself? Men who live by hard work must be strong and healthy, and they should have strong and healthy children. . . . Do I speak truly?"

"Yes," assented the listeners.

"But all this will never happen," says Yashka, becoming rather frightened at the prospect held out to him by the teacher. "She is healthy, and I cannot have reached the child . . . She is a devil—a hag!" he shouts angrily. "I would . . . She will eat me away as rust eats iron."

"I understand, Yakov, that you cannot help beating your wife," the teacher's sad and thoughtful voice again breaks in. "You have many reasons for doing so . . . It is your wife's character that causes you to beat her so incautiously . . . But your own dark and sad life . . ."

"You are right!" shouts Yakov. "We live in darkness, like the chimney-sweep when he is in the chimney!"

"You are angry with your life, but your wife is patient; the closest relation to you—your wife, and you make her suffer for this, simply because you are stronger than she. She is always with you, and cannot get away. Don't you see how absurd you are?"

"That is so. . . . Devil take it! But what shall I do? Am I not a man?"

"Just so! You are a man. . . . I only wish to tell you that if you cannot help beating her, then beat her carefully and always remember that you may injure her health or that of the child. It is not good to beat pregnant women . . . on their belly or on their sides and chests. . . . Beat her, say, on the neck . . . or else take a rope and beat her on some soft place . . ."

The orator finished his speech and looked upon his hearers with his dark, pathetic eyes, seeming to apologize to them for some unknown crime.

The public understands it. They understand the

morale of the creature who was once a man, the *morale* of the public-house and much misfortune.

"Well, brother Yashka, did you understand? See how true it is!"

Yakov understood that to beat her incautiously might be injurious to his wife. He is silent, replying to his companions' jokes with confused smiles.

"Then again, what is a wife?" philosophizes the baker, Mokei Anisimoff. "A wife . . . is a friend . . . if we look at the matter in that way. She is like a chain, chained to you for life . . . and you are both just like galley slaves. And if you try to get away from her, you cannot, you feel the chain . . ."

"Wait," says Yakovleff; "but you beat your wife too."

"Did I say that I did not? I beat her. . . . There is nothing else handy. . . . Do you expect me to beat the wall with my fist when my patience is exhausted?"

"I feel just like that too. . ." says Yakov.

"How hard and difficult our life is, my brothers! There is no real rest for us anywhere!"

"And even you beat your wife by mistake," some one remarks humorously. And thus they speak till far on in the night or till they have quarrelled, the usual result of drink or of passions engendered by such discussions.

The rain beats on the windows, and outside the cold wind is blowing. The eating-house is close with tobacco smoke, but it is warm, while the street is cold and wet. Now and then, the wind beats threateningly on the windows of the eating-house, as if bidding these men to come out and be scattered like dust over the face of the earth. Sometimes a stifled and hopeless groan is heard in its howling which again is drowned by cold, cruel laughter. This music fills one with dark, sad thoughts of the approaching winter, with its accursed short, sunless days and long nights, of the necessity of possessing warm garments and plenty to eat. It is hard to sleep through the long winter nights on an empty stomach. Winter is approaching. Yes, it is approaching. . . . How to live?

These gloomy forebodings created a strong thirst among the inhabitants of the main street, and the sighs of the "creatures that once were men" increased with the wrinkles on their brows, their voices became thick and their behavior to each other more blunt. And brutal crimes were committed among them, and the roughness of these poor unfortunate outcasts was apt to increase at the approach of that inexorable enemy, who transformed all their lives into one cruel farce. But this enemy could not be captured because it was invisible.

Then they began beating each other brutally, and drank till they had drunk everything which they could pawn to the indulgent Vaviloff. And thus they passed the autumn days in open wickedness, in suffering which was eating their hearts out, unable to rise out of this vicious life and in dread of the still crueller days of winter.

Kuvalda in such cases came to their assistance with his philosophy.

"Don't lose your temper, brothers, everything has an end, this is the chief characteristic of life. The winter will pass, summer will follow . . . a glorious time, when the very sparrows are filled with rejoicing." But his speeches did not have any effect—a mouthful of even the freshest and purest water will not satisfy a hungry man.

Deacon Taras also tried to amuse the people by singing his songs and relating his tales. He was more successful, and sometimes his endeavors ended in a wild and glorious orgy at the eating-house. They sang, laughed and danced, and for hours behaved like madmen. After this they again fell into a despairing mood, sitting at the tables of the eating-house, in the black smoke of the lamp and the tobacco; sad and tattered, speaking lazily to each other, listening to the wild howling of the wind, and thinking how they could get enough vodki to deaden their senses.

And their hand was against every man, and every man's hand against them.

PART II

ALL things are relative in this world, and a man cannot sink into any condition so bad that it could not be worse. One day, toward the end of September, Captain Aristid Kuvalda was sitting, as was his custom, on the bench near the door of the dosshouse, looking at the stone building built by the merchant Petunikoff close to Vaviloff's eating-house, and thinking deeply. This building, which was partly surrounded by woods, served the purpose of a candle factory.

Painted red, as if with blood, it looked like a cruel machine which, though not working, opened a row of deep, hungry, gaping jaws, as if ready to devour and swallow anything. The gray wooden eating-house of Vaviloff, with its bent roof covered with patches, leaned against one of the brick walls of the factory, and seemed as if it were some large form of parasite clinging to it. The Captain was thinking that they would very soon be making new houses to replace the old building. "They will destroy the dosshouse even," he reflected. "It will be necessary to look out for another, but such a cheap one is not to be found. It seems a great pity to have to leave a place to which one is accustomed, though it will be necessary to go, simply because some merchant or other thinks of manufacturing candles and soap." And the Captain felt that if he could only make the life of such an enemy miserable, even temporarily, oh! with what pleasure he would do it!

Yesterday, Ivan Andreyevitch Petunikoff was in the dosshouse yard with his son and an architect. They measured the yard and put small wooden sticks in various places, which, after the exit of Petunikoff and at the order of the Captain, Meteor took out and threw away. To the eyes of the Captain this merchant appeared small and thin. He wore a long garment like a frock-coat, a velvet cap, and high, well-cleaned boots. He had a thin face with prominent cheek-bones, a wedge-shaped grayish beard, and a high forehead seamed with wrinkles from beneath which shone two narrow, blinking, and observant gray eyes . . . a sharp, gristly nose, a small mouth with thin lips . . .

altogether his appearance was pious, rapacious, and respectably wicked.

"Cursed cross-bred fox and pig!" swore the Captain under his breath, recalling his first meeting with Petunikoff. The merchant came with one of the town council-lors to buy the house, and seeing the Captain asked his companion:

"Is this your lodger?"

And from that day, a year and a half ago, there has been keen competition among the inhabitants of the dosshouse as to which can swear the hardest at the merchant. And last night there was a "slight skirmish with hot words," as the Captain called it, between Petunikoff and himself. Having dismissed the archi-tect the merchant approached the Captain.

"What are you hatching?" asked he, putting his hand to his cap, perhaps to adjust it, perhaps as a salutation.

"What are you plotting?" answered the Captain in the same tone. He moved his chin so that his beard trem-bled a little; a non-exacting person might have taken it for a bow; otherwise it only expressed the desire of the Captain to move his pipe from one corner of his mouth to the other. "You see, having plenty of money, I can afford to sit hatching it. Money is a good thing, and I possess it," the Captain chaffed the merchant, casting cunning glances at him. "It means that you serve money, and not money you," went on Kuvalda, desiring at the same time to punch the merchant's belly.

"Isn't it all the same? Money makes life comfortable, but no money," . . . and the merchant looked at the Captain with a feigned expression of suffering. The other's upper lip curled, and exposed large, wolf-like teeth.

"With brains and a conscience, it is possible to live without it. Men only acquire riches when they cease to listen to their conscience . . . the less conscience the more money !"

"Just so; but then there are men who have neither money nor conscience."

"Were you just like what you are now when you were young?" asked Kuvalda simply. The other's nostrils twitched. Ivan Andreyevitch sighed, passed his hand over his eyes and said:

"Oh! When I was young I had to undergo a great many difficulties . . . Work! Oh! I did work !"

"And you cheated, too, I suppose?"

"People like you? Nobles? I should just think so! They used to grovel at my feet !"

"You only went in for robbing, not murder, I suppose?" asked the Captain. Petunikoff turned pale, and hastily changed the subject.

"You are a bad host. You sit while your guest stands."

"Let him sit, too," said Kuvalda.

"But what am I to sit on?"

"On the earth . . . it will take any rubbish . . ."

"You are the proof of that," said Petunikoff quietly, while his eyes shot forth poisonous glances.

And he went away, leaving Kuvalda under the pleasant impression that the merchant was afraid of him. If he were not afraid of him he would long ago have evicted him from the dosshouse. But then he would think twice before turning him out, because of the five roubles a month. And the Captain gazed with pleasure at Petunikoff's back as he slowly retreated from the court-yard. Following him with his eyes, he noticed how the merchant passed the factory and disappeared into the wood, and he wished very much that he might fall and break all his bones. He sat imagining many horrible forms of disaster while watching Petunikoff, who was descending the hill into the wood like a spider going into its web. Last night he even imagined that the wood gave way before the merchant and he fell . . . but afterward he found that he had only been dreaming.

And to-day, as always, the red building stands out before the eyes of Aristid Kuvalda, so plain, so massive, and clinging so strongly to the earth, that it seems to be sucking away all its life. It appears to be laughing coldly at the Captain with its gaping walls. The sun pours its rays on them as generously as it does on the miserable hovels of the main street.

"Devil take the thing!" exclaimed the Captain, thoughtfully measuring the walls of the factory with his eyes. "If only . . ." Trembling with excitement at the thought that had just entered his mind Aristid Kuvalda jumped up and ran to Vaviloff's eating-house muttering to himself all the time.

Vaviloff met him at the bar and gave him a friendly welcome.

"I wish your honor good health!" He was of middle height and had a bald head, gray hair, and straight mustaches like tooth-brushes. Upright and neat in his clean jacket, he showed by every movement that he was an old soldier.

"Egorka, show me the lease and plan of your house," demanded Kuvalda impatiently.

"I have shown it you before." Vaviloff looked up suspiciously and closely scanned the Captain's face.

"Show it me!" shouted the Captain, striking the bar with his fist and sitting down on a stool close by.

"But why?" asked Vaviloff, knowing that it was better to keep his wits about him when Kuvalda got excited.

"You fool! Bring it at once."

Vaviloff rubbed his forehead, and turned his eyes to the ceiling in a tired way.

"Where are those papers of yours?"

There was no answer to this on the ceiling, so the old sergeant looked down at the floor, and began drumming with his fingers on the bar in a worried and thoughtful manner.

"It's no good your making wry faces!" shouted the Captain, for he had no great affection for him, thinking that a former soldier should rather have become a thief than an eating-house keeper.

"Oh! Yes! Aristid Fomich, I remember now. They were left at the High Court of Justice at the time when I came into possession."

"Get along, Egorka! It is to your own interest to show me the plan, the title-deeds, and everything you have immediately. You will probably clear at least a hundred roubles over this, do you understand?"

Vaviloff did not understand at all; but the Captain spoke in such a serious and convincing tone that the sergeant's eyes burned with curiosity, and, telling him that he would see if the papers were in his desk, he went through the door behind the bar. Two minutes later he returned with the papers in his hand, and an expression of extreme astonishment on his face.

"Here they are; the deeds about the damned houses!"

"Ah! You . . . vagabond! And you pretend to have been a soldier, too!" And Kuvalda did not cease to belabor him with his tongue, as he snatched the blue parchment from his hands. Then, spreading the papers out in front of him, and excited all the more by Vaviloff's inquisitiveness, the Captain began reading and bellowing at the same time. At last he got up resolutely, and went to the door, leaving all the papers on the bar, and saying to Vaviloff:

"Wait! Don't lift them!"

Vaviloff gathered them up, put them into the cashbox, and locked it, then felt the lock with his hand, to see if it were secure. After that, he scratched his bald head, thoughtfully, and went up on the roof of the eating-house. There he saw the Captain measuring the front of the house, and watched him anxiously, as he snapped his fingers, and began measuring the same line over again. Vaviloff's face lit up suddenly, and he smiled happily.

"Aristid Fomich, is it possible?" he shouted, when the Captain came opposite to him.

"Of course it is possible. There is more than one short in the front alone, and as to the depth I shall see immediately."

"The depth . . . seventy-three feet."

"What? Have you guessed, you shaved, ugly face?"

"Of course, Aristid Fomich! If you have eyes you can see a thing or two," shouted Vaviloff joyfully.

A few minutes afterward they sat side by side in Vaviloff's parlor, and the Captain was engaged in drinking large quantities of beer.

"And so all the walls of the factory stand on your ground," said he to the eating-house keeper. "Now, mind you show no mercy! The teacher will be here presently, and we will get him to draw up a petition to the court. As to the amount of the damages you will name a very moderate sum in order not to waste money in deed stamps, but we will ask to have the factory knocked down. This, you see, donkey, is the result of trespassing on other people's property. It is a splendid piece of luck for you. We will force him to have the place smashed, and I can tell you it will be an expensive job for him. Off with you to the court. Bring pressure to bear on Judas. We will calculate how much it will take to break the factory down to its very foundations. We will make an estimate of it all, counting the time it will take too, and we will make honest Judas pay two thousand roubles besides."

"He will never give it!" cried Vaviloff, but his eyes shone with a greedy light.

"You lie! He will give it . . . Use your brains. . . What else can he do? But look here, Egorka, mind you, don't go in for doing it on the cheap. They are sure to try to buy you off. Don't sell yourself cheap. They will probably use threats, but rely upon us. . . ."

The Captain's eyes were alight with happiness, and

his face red with excitement. He worked upon Vaviloff's greed, and urging upon him the importance of
immediate action in the matter, went away in a very
joyful and happy frame of mind.

*   *   *   *   *

In the evening everyone was told of the Captain's
discovery, and they all began to discuss Petunikoff's
future predicament, painting in vivid colors his excitement and astonishment on the day the court messenger
handed him the copy of the summons. The Captain
felt himself quite a hero. He was happy and all his
friends highly pleased. The heap of dark and tattered
figures that lay in the courtyard made noisy demonstra-
tions of pleasure. They all knew the merchant, Petunikoff, who passed them very often, contemptuously
turning up his eyes and giving them no more attention
than he bestowed on the other heaps of rubbish lying on
the ground. He was well fed, and that exasperated
them still more; and now how splendid it was that one
of themselves had struck a hard blow at the selfish merchant's purse! It gave them all the greatest pleasure.
The Captain's discovery was a powerful instrument in
their hands. Every one of them felt keen animosity
toward all those who were well fed and well dressed, but
in some of them this feeling was only beginning to
develop. Burning interest was felt by those "creatures
that once were men" in the prospective fight between
Kuvalda and Petunikoff, which they already saw in
imagination.

For a fortnight the inhabitants of the dosshouse awaited the further development of events, but Petunikoff never once visited the building. It was known that he was not in town, and that the copy of the petition had not yet been handed to him. Kuvalda raged at the delays of the civil court. It is improbable that anyone had ever awaited the merchant with such impatience as did this bare-footed brigade.

"He isn't even thinking of coming, the wretch! . . ."

"That means that he does not love me!" sang Deacon Taras, leaning his chin on his hand and casting a humorous glance toward the mountain.

At last Petunikoff appeared. He came in a respectable cart with his son playing the rôle of groom. The latter was a red-cheeked, nice-looking youngster, in a long square-cut overcoat. He wore smoked eyeglasses. They tied the horse to an adjoining tree, the son took the measuring instrument out of his pocket and gave it to his father, and they began to measure the ground. Both were silent and worried.

"Aha!" shouted the Captain gleefully.

All those who were in the dosshouse at the moment came out to look at them and expressed themselves loudly and freely in reference to the matter.

"What does the habit of thieving mean? A man may sometimes make a big mistake when he steals, standing to lose more than he gets," said the Captain, causing much laughter among his staff and eliciting various murmurs of assent.

"Take care, you devil!" shouted Petunikoff, "lest I have you in the police court for your words!"

"You can do nothing to me without witnesses . . . Your son cannot give evidence on your side" . . . the Captain warned him.

"Look out all the same, you old wretch, you may be found guilty too!" And Petunikoff shook his fist at him. His son, deeply engrossed in his calculations, took no notice of the dark group of men, who were taking such a wicked delight in adding to his father's discomfiture. He did not even once look in their direction.

"The young spider has himself well in hand," remarked Abyedok, watching young Petunikoff's every movement and action. Having taken all the measurements he desired, Ivan Andreyevitch knit his brows, got into the cart, and drove away. His son went with a firm step into Vaviloff's eating-house, and disappeared behind the door.

"Ho, ho! That's a determined young thief! . . . What will happen next, I wonder . . . ?" asked Kuvalda.

"Next? Young Petunikoff will buy out Egor Vaviloff," said Abyedok with conviction, and smacked his lips as if the idea gave him great pleasure.

"And you are glad of that?" Kuvalda asked him gravely.

"I am always pleased to see human calculations miscarry," explained Abyedok, rolling his eyes and rubbing his hands with delight. The Captain spat angrily on the ground and was silent. They all stood in front of the tumble-down building, and silently watched the doors of the eating-house. More than an hour passed thus. Then the doors opened and Petunikoff came out as silently as he had entered. He stopped for a moment, coughed, turned up the collar of his coat, glanced at the men, who were following all his movements with their eyes, and then went up the street toward the town.

The Captain watched him for a moment, and turning to Abyedok said smilingly:

"Probably you were right after all, you son of a scorpion and a wood-louse! You nose out every evil thing. Yes, the face of that young swindler shows that he has got what he wanted. . . . I wonder how much Egorka has got out of them. He has evidently taken something. . . He is just the same sort of rogue that they are . . . they are all tarred with the same brush. He has got some money, and I'm damned if I did not arrange the whole thing for him! It is best to own my folly. . . Yes, life is against us all, brothers . . . and even when you spit upon those nearest to you, the spittle rebounds and hits your own face."

Having satisfied himself with this reflection, the worthy Captain looked round upon his staff. Every one of them was disappointed, because they all knew that something they did not expect had taken place between Petunikoff and Vaviloff, and they all felt that they had been insulted. The feeling that one is unable to injure anyone is worse than the feeling that one is unable to do good, because to do harm is far easier and simpler.

"Well, why are we loitering here? We have nothing more to wait for . . . except the reward that I shall get out—out of Egorka,. . ." said the Captain, looking angrily at the eating-house. "So our peaceful life under the roof of Judas has come to an end. Judas will now turn us out. . . . So do not say that I have not warned you."

Kanets smiled sadly.

"What are you laughing at, jailer?" Kuvalda asked.

"Where shall I go then?"

"That, my soul, is a question that fate will settle for you, so do not worry," said the Captain thoughtfully, entering the dosshouse. "The creatures that once were men" followed him.

"We can do nothing but await the critical moment," said the Captain, walking about among them. "When they turn us out we shall seek a new place for ourselves, but at present there is no use spoiling our life by thinking of it . . . In times of crisis one becomes energetic . . . and if life were fuller of them and every moment of it so arranged that we were compelled to tremble for our lives all the time . . . By God! life would be livelier and even fuller of interest and energy than it is!"

"That means that people would all go about cutting one another's throats," explained Abyedok smilingly.

"Well, what about it?" asked the Captain angrily. He did not like to hear his thoughts illustrated.

"Oh! Nothing! When a person wants to get anywhere quickly he whips up the horses, but of course it needs fire to make engines go . . ."

"Well, let everything go to the Devil as quickly as possible. I'm sure I should be pleased if the earth suddenly opened up or was burned or destroyed somehow . . . only I were left to the last in order to see the others consumed . . ."

"Ferocious creature!" smiled Abyedok.

"Well, what of that? I . . . I was once a man . . . now I am an outcast . . . that means I have no obligations. It means that I am free to spit on everyone. The nature of my present life means the rejection of my past . . . giving up all relations toward men who are well fed and well dressed, and who look upon me with contempt because I am inferior to them in the matter of feeding or dressing. I must develop something new within myself, do you understand? Something that will make Judas Petunikoff and his kind tremble and perspire before me!"

"Ah! You have a courageous tongue!" jeered Abyedok.

"Yes . . . You miser!" And Kuvalda looked at him contemptuously. "What do you understand? What do you know? Are you able to think? But I have thought and I have read . . . books of which you could not have understood one word."

"Of course! One cannot eat soup out of one's hand . . . But though you have read and thought, and I have not done that or anything else, we both seem to have got into pretty much the same condition, don't we?"

"Go to the Devil!" shouted Kuvalda. His conversations with Abyedok always ended thus. When the teacher was absent his speeches, as a rule, fell on the empty air, and received no attention, and he knew this, but still he could not help speaking. And now, having quarrelled with his companion, he felt rather deserted; but, still longing for conversation, he turned to Simtsoff with the following question: "And you, Aleksei Maksimovitch, where will you lay your gray head?"

The old man smiled good-humoredly, rubbed his hands, and replied, "I do not know . . . . I will see. One does not require much, just a little drink."

"Plain but honorable fare!" the Captain said. Simtsoff was silent, only adding that he would find a place sooner than any of them, because women loved him. This was true. The old man had, as a rule, two or three prostitutes, who kept him on their very scant earnings. They very often beat him, but he took this stoically. They somehow never beat him too much, probably because they pitied him. He was a great lover of women, and said they were the cause of all his misfortunes. The character of his relations toward them was confirmed by the appearance of his clothes, which, as a rule, were tidy, and cleaner than those of his companions. And now, sitting at the door of the dosshouse, he boastingly related that for a long time past Redka had been asking him to go and live with her, but he had not gone because he did not want to part with the company. They heard this with jealous interest. They all knew Redka. She lived very near the town, almost below the mountain. Not long ago, she had been in prison for theft. She was a retired nurse; a tall, stout peasant woman with a face marked by smallpox, but with very pretty, though always drunken, eyes.

"Just look at the old devil!" swore Abyedok, looking at Simtsoff, who was smiling in a self-satisfied way.

"And do you know why they love me? Because I know how to cheer up their souls."

"Do you?" inquired Kuvalda.

"And I can make them pity me. . . . And a woman, when she pities! Go and weep to her, and ask her to kill you . . . she will pity you—and she will kill you."

"I feel inclined to commit a murder," declared Martyanoff, laughing his dull laugh.

"Upon whom?" asked Abyedok, edging away from him.

"It's all the same to me . . . Petunikoff . . . Egorka . . . or even you!"

"And why?" inquired Kuvalda.

"I want to go to Siberia . . . I have had enough of this vile life . . . one learns how to live there!"

"Yes, they have a particularly good way of teaching in Siberia," agreed the Captain sadly.

They spoke no more of Petunikoff, or of the turning out of the inhabitants of the dosshouse. They all knew that they would have to leave soon, therefore they did not think the matter worth discussion. It would do no good, and besides the weather was not very cold though the rains had begun . . . and it would be possible to sleep on the ground anywhere outside the town. They sat in a circle on the grass and conversed about all sorts of things, discussing one subject after another, and listening attentively even to the poor speakers in order to make the time pass; keeping quiet was as dull as listening. This society of "creatures that once were men" had one fine characteristic—no one of them endeavored to make out that he was better than the others, nor compelled the others to acknowledge his superiority.

The August sun seemed to set their tatters on fire as

they sat with their backs and uncovered heads exposed to it . . . a chaotic mixture of the vegetable, mineral, and animal kingdoms. In the corners of the yard the tall steppe grass grew luxuriantly. . . . . Nothing else grew there but some dingy vegetables, not attractive even to those who nearly always felt the pangs of hunger.

*   *   *   *   *

The following was the scene that took place in Vaviloff's eating-house.

Young Petunikoff entered slowly, took off his hat, looked around him, and said to the eating-house keeper:

"Egor Terentievitch Vaviloff? Are you he?"

"I am," answered the sergeant, leaning on the bar with both arms as if intending to jump over it.

"I have some business with you," said Petunikoff.

"Delighted. Please come this way to my private room."

They went in and sat down, the guest on the couch and his host on the chair opposite to him. In one corner a lamp was burning before a gigantic icon, and on the wall at the other side there were several oil lamps. They were well kept and shone as if they were new. The room, which contained a number of boxes and a variety of furniture, smelt of tobacco, sour cabbage, and olive oil. Petunikoff looked around him and made a face. Vaviloff looked at the icon, and then they looked simultaneously at one another, and both seemed to be favorably impressed. Petunikoff liked Vaviloff's frankly thievish eyes, and Vaviloff was pleased with the open, cold, determined face of Petunikoff, with its large cheeks and white teeth.

"Of course you already know me, and I presume you guess what I am going to say to you," began Petunikoff.

"About the lawsuit? . . . I presume?" remarked the ex-sergeant respectfully.

"Exactly! I am glad to see that you are not beating about the bush, but going straight to the point like a business man," said Petunikoff encouragingly.

"I am a soldier," answered Vaviloff, with a modest air.

"That is easily seen, and I am sure we shall be able to finish this job without much trouble."

"Just so."

"Good! You have the law on your side, and will, of course, win your case. I want to tell you this at the very beginning."

"I thank you most humbly," said the sergeant, rubbing his eyes in order to hide the smile in them.

"But tell me, why did you make the acquaintance of your future neighbors like this through the law courts?"

Vaviloff shrugged his shoulders and did not answer.

"It would have been better to come straight to us and settle the matter peacefully, eh? What do you think?"

"That would have been better, of course, but you see there is a difficulty . . . I did not follow my own wishes, but those of others . . . I learned afterward that it would have been better if . . . but it was too late."

"Oh! I suppose some lawyer taught you this?"

"Someone of that sort."

"Aha! Do you wish to settle the affair peacefully,"

"With all my heart!" cried the soldier.

Petunikoff was silent for a moment, then looked at him, and suddenly asked, coldly and dryly, "And why do you wish to do so?"

Vaviloff did not expect such a question, and therefore had no reply ready. In his opinion the question was quite unworthy of any attention, and so he laughed at young Petunikoff.

"That is easy to understand. Men like to live peacefully with one another."

"But," interrupted Petunikoff, "that is not exactly the reason why. As far as I can see, you do not distinctly understand why you wish to be reconciled to us . . . I will tell you."

The soldier was a little surprised. This youngster, dressed in a check suit, in which he looked ridiculous, spoke as if he were Colonel Rakshin, who used to knock three of the unfortunate soldier's teeth out every time he was angry.

"You want to be friends with us because we should be such useful neighbors to you . . . because there will be not less than a hundred and fifty workmen in our factory, and in course of time even more. If a hundred men come and drink one glass at your place, after receiving their weekly wages, that means that you will sell every month four hundred glasses more than you sell at present. This is, of course, the lowest estimate . . . and then you have the eating-house besides. You are not a fool, and you can understand for yourself what profitable neighbors we shall be."

"That is true," Vaviloff nodded "I knew that before."

"Well, what then?" asked the merchant loudly.

"Nothing . . . Let us be friends!"

"It is nice to see that you have decided so quickly. Look here, I have already prepared a notification to the court of the withdrawal of the summons against my father. Here it is; read it, and sign it."

Vaviloff looked at his companion with his round eyes and shivered, as if experiencing an unpleasant sensation.

"Pardon me . . . sign it? And why?"

"There is no difficulty about it . . . write your Christian name and surname and nothing more," explained Petunikoff, pointing obligingly with his finger to the place for the signature.

"Oh! It is not that . . . I was alluding to the compensation I was to get for my ground."

"But then this ground is of no use to you," said Petunikoff calmly.

"But it is mine!" exclaimed the soldier.

"Of course, and how much do you want for it?"

"Well, say the amount stated in the document," said Vaviloff boldly.

"Six hundred!" and Petunikoff smiled softly. "You are a funny fellow!"

"The law is on my side . . . I can even demand two thousand. I can insist on your pulling down the building . . . and enforce it too. That is why my claim is so small. I demand that you should pull it down!"

"Very well. Probably we shall do so . . . after three

years, and after having dragged you into enormous law expenses. And then, having paid up, we shall open our public-house, and you will be ruined . . . annihilated like the Swedes at Poltava. We shall see that you are ruined . . . we will take good care of that. We could have begun to arrange about a public-house now, but you see our time is valuable, and besides we are sorry for you. Why should we take the bread out of your mouth without any reason?"

. Egor Terentievitch looked at his guest, clenching his teeth, and felt that he was master of the situation, and held his fate in his hands. Vaviloff was full of pity for himself at having to deal with this calm, cruel figure in the checked suit.

"And being such a near neighbor you might have gained a good deal by helping us, and we should have remembered it too. Even now, for instance, I should advise you to open a small shop for tobacco, you know, bread, cucumbers, and so on. . . . All these are sure to be in great demand."

Vaviloff listened, and being a clever man, knew that to throw himself upon the enemy's generosity was the better plan. It was as well to begin from the beginning, and, not knowing what else to do to relieve his mind, the soldier began to swear at Kuvalda.

"Curses be upon your head, you drunken rascal! May the Devil take you!"

"Do you mean the lawyer who composed your petition?" asked Petunikoff calmly, and added, with a sigh, "I have no doubt he would have landed you in rather an awkward fix . . . had we not taken pity upon you."

"Ah!" And the angry soldier raised his hand. "There are two of them . . . One of them discovered it, the other wrote the petition, the accursed reporter!"

"Why the reporter?"

"He writes for the papers . . . He is one of your lodgers . . . there they all are outside . . . Clear them away, for Christ's sake! The robbers! They disturb and annoy everyone in the street. One cannot live for them . . . And they are all desperate fellows . . . You had better take care, or else they will rob or burn you . . ."

"And this reporter, who is he?" asked Petunikoff, with interest.

"He? A drunkard. He was a teacher, but was dismissed. He drank everything he possessed . . . and now he writes for the papers and composes petitions. He is a very wicked man!"

"H'm! And did he write your petition, too? I suppose it was he who discovered the flaws in the building. The beams were not rightly put in?"

"He did! I know it for a fact! The dog! He read it aloud in here and boasted, 'Now I have caused Petunikoff some loss!'"

"Ye—es. . . . Well, then, do you want to be reconciled?"

"To be reconciled?" The soldier lowered his head and thought. "Ah! This is a hard life!" said he, in a querulous voice, scratching his head.

"One must learn by experience," Petunikoff reassured him, lighting a cigarette.

"Learn . . . It is not that, my dear sir; but don't

you see there is no freedom? Don't you see what a life I lead? I live in fear and trembling . . . I am refused the freedom so desirable to me in my movements, and I fear this ghost of a teacher will write about me in the papers. Sanitary inspectors will be called for . . . fines will have to be paid . . . or else your lodgers will set fire to the place or rob and kill me . . . I am powerless against them. They are not the least afraid of the police, and they like going to prison, because they get their food for nothing there."

"But then we will have them turned out if we come to terms with you," promised Petunikoff.

"What shall we arrange, then?" asked Vaviloff sadly and seriously.

"Tell me your terms."

"Well, give me the six hundred mentioned in the claim."

"Won't you take a hundred roubles?" asked the merchant calmly, looking attentively at his companion, and smiling softly. "I will not give you one rouble more," . . . he added.

After this, he took out his eyeglasses and began cleaning them with his handkerchief. Vaviloff looked at him sadly and respectfully. The calm face of Petunikoff, his gray eyes and clear complexion, every line of his thickset body betokened self-confidence and a well-balanced mind. Vaviloff also liked Petunikoff's straightforward manner of addressing him without any pretensions, as if he were his own brother, though Vaviloff understood well enough that he was his superior, he being only a soldier. Looking at him, he grew fonder and fonder of him, and, forgetting for a moment the matter in hand, respectfully asked Petunikoff:

"Where did you study?"

'In the technological institute. Why?" answered the other, smiling:

"Nothing. Only . . . excuse me!" The soldier lowered his head, and then suddenly exclaimed, "What a splendid thing education is! Science—light. My brother, I am as stupid as an owl before the sun . . . Your honor, let us finish this job."

With an air of decision he stretched out his hand to Petunikoff and said:

"Well, five hundred?"

"Not more than one hundred roubles, Egor Terentievitch."

Petunikoff shrugged his shoulders as if sorry at being unable to give more, and touched the soldier's hairy hand with his long white fingers. They soon ended the matter, for the soldier gave in quickly and met Petunikoff's wishes. And when Vaviloff had received the hundred roubles and signed the paper, he threw the pen down on the table and said bitterly:

"Now I will have a nice time! They will laugh at me, they will cry shame on me, the devils!"

"But you tell them that I paid all your claim," suggested Petunikoff, calmly puffing out clouds of smoke and watching them float upward.

"But do you think they will believe it? They are as clever swindlers if not worse . . ."

Vaviloff stopped himself in time before making the intended comparison, and looked at the merchant's son in terror. The other smoked on, and seemed to be absorbed in that occupation. He went away soon, promising to destroy the nest of vagabonds. Vaviloff looked after him and sighed, feeling as if he would like to shout some insult at the young man who was going with such firm steps toward the steep road, encumbered with its ditches and heaps of rubbish.

In the evening the Captain appeared in the eating-house. His eyebrows were knit and his fist clenched. Vaviloff smiled at him in a guilty manner.

"Well, worthy descendant of Judas and Cain, tell us . . ."

"They decided" . . . said Vaviloff, sighing and lowering his eyes.

"I don't doubt it; how many silver pieces did you receive?"

"Four hundred roubles" . . .

"Of course you are lying . . . But all the better for me. Without any further words, Egorka, ten per cent. of it for my discovery, four per cent. to the teacher for writing the petition, one 'vedro' of vodki to all of us, and refreshments all round. Give me the money now, the vodki and refreshments will do at eight o'clock."

Vaviloff turned purple with rage, and stared at Kuvalda with wide-open eyes.

"This is humbug! This is robbery! I will do nothing of the sort. What do you mean, Aristid Fomich? Keep your appetite for the next feast! I am not afraid of you now . . ."

Kuvalda looked at the clock.

"I give you ten minutes, Egorka, for your idiotic talk.

Finish your nonsense by that time and give me what I demand. If you don't I will devour you! Kanets has sold you something? Did you read in the paper about the theft at Basoff's house? Do you understand? You won't have time to hide anything, we will not let you . . . and this very night . . . do you understand?"

"Why, Aristid Fomich?" sobbed the discomfited merchant.

"No more words! Did you understand or not?"

Tall, gray, and imposing, Kuvalda spoke in half whispers, and his deep bass voice rang through the house. Vaviloff always feared him because he was not only a retired military man, but a man who had nothing to lose. But now Kuvalda appeared before him in a new rôle. He did not speak much, and jocosely as usual, but spoke in the tone of a commander, who was convinced of the other's guilt. And Vaviloff felt that the Captain could and would ruin him with the greatest pleasure. He must needs bow before this power. Nevertheless, the soldier thought of trying him once more. He sighed deeply, and began with apparent calmness:

"It is truly said that a man's sin will find him out . . . I lied to you, Aristid Fomich, . . . I tried to be cleverer than I am . . . I only received one hundred roubles."

"Go on!" said Kuvalda.

"And not four hundred as I told you . . . That means . . ."

"It does not mean anything. It is all the same to me whether you lied or not. You owe me sixty-five roubles. That is not much, eh?"

"Oh! my Lord! Aristid Fomich! I have always been attentive to your honor and done my best to please you."

"Drop all that, Egorka, grandchild of Judas!"

"All right! I will give it you . . . only God will punish you for this. . . ."

"Silence! You rotten pimple of the earth!" shouted the Captain, rolling his eyes. "He has punished me enough already in forcing me to have conversation with you. . . . I will kill you on the spot like a fly!"

He shook his fist in Vaviloff's face and ground his teeth till they nearly broke.

After he had gone Vaviloff began smiling and winking to himself. Then two large drops rolled down his cheeks. They were grayish, and they hid themselves in his moustache, while two others followed them. Then Vaviloff went into his own room and stood before the icon, stood there without praying, immovable, with the salt tears running down his wrinkled brown cheeks. . . .

*   *   *   *   *

Deacon Taras, who, as a rule, loved to loiter in the woods and fields, proposed to the "creatures that once were men" that they should go together into the fields, and there drink Vaviloff's vodki in the bosom of Nature. But the Captain and all the rest swore at the Deacon, and decided to drink it in the courtyard.

"One, two, three," counted Aristid Fomich; "our full number is thirty, the teacher is not here . . . but probably many other outcasts will come. Let us calculate, say, twenty persons, and to every person two-and-a-half cucumbers, a pound of bread, and a pound of meat . . . That won't be bad! One bottle of vodki each, and there is plenty of sour cabbage, and three water-melons. I ask you, what the devil could you want more, my scoundrel friends? Now, then, let us prepare to devour Egorka Vaviloff, because all this is his blood and body!"

They spread some old clothes on the ground, setting the delicacies and the drink on them, and sat around the feast, solemnly and quietly, but almost unable to control the craving for drink that was shining in their eyes.

The evening began to fall, and its shadows were cast on the human refuse of the earth in the courtyard of the dosshouse; the last rays of the sun illumined the roof of the tumble-down building. The night was cold and silent.

"Let us begin, brothers!" commanded the Captain. "How many cups have we? Six . . . and there are thirty of us! Aleksei Maksimovitch, pour it out. Is it ready? Now then, the first toast. . . . Come along!"

They drank and shouted, and began to eat.

"The teacher is not here. . . I have not seen him for three days. Has anyone seen him?" asked Kuvalda.

"No one."

"It is unlike . . . Let us drink to the health of Aristid Kuvalda . . . the only friend who has never deserted me for one moment of my life! Devil take him all the same! I might have had something to wear had he left my society at least for a little while."

"You are bitter . . ." said Abyedok, and coughed.

The Captain, with his feeling of superiority to the others, never talked with his mouth full.

Having drunk twice, the company began to grow merry; the food was grateful to them.

Paltara Taras expressed his desire to hear a tale, but the Deacon was arguing with Kubaroff over his preferring thin women to stout ones, and paid no attention to his friend's request. He was asserting his views on the subject to Kubaroff with all the decision of a man who was deeply convinced in his own mind.

The foolish face of Meteor, who was lying on the ground, showed that he was drinking in the Deacon's strong words.

Martyanoff sat, clasping his large hairy hands round his knees, looking silently and sadly at the bottle of vodki and pulling his moustache as if trying to bite it with his teeth, while Abyedok was teasing Tyapa.

"I have seen you watching the place where your money is hidden!"

"That is your luck," shouted Tyapa.

"I will go halves with you, brother."

"All right, take it and welcome."

Kuvalda felt angry with these men. Among them all there was not one worthy of hearing his oratory or of understanding him.

"I wonder where the teacher is?" he asked loudly.

Martyanoff looked at him and said, "He will come soon" . . .

"I am positive that he will come, but he won't come in a carriage. Let us drink to your future health. If you kill any rich man go halves with me . . . then I shall go to America, brother. To those . . . what do you call them? Limpas? Pampas? I will go there, and I will work my way until I become the President of the United States, and then I will challenge the whole of Europe to war and I will blow it up! I will buy the army . . . in Europe that is—I will invite the French, the Germans, the Turks, and so on, and I will kill them by the hands of their own relatives . . . Just as Elia Marumets bought a Tartar with a Tartar. With money it would be possible even for Elia to destroy the whole of Europe and to take Judas Petunikoff for his valet. He would go. . . Give him a hundred roubles a month and he would go! But he would be a bad valet, because he would soon begin to steal . . ."

"Now, besides that, the thin woman is better than the stout one, because she costs one less," said the Deacon, convincingly. "My first Deaconess used to buy twelve arshins for her clothes, but the second one only ten. . . . And so on even in the matter of provisions and food."

Paltara Taras smiled guiltily. Turning his head towards the Deacon and looking straight at him, he said, with conviction:

"I had a wife once, too."

"Oh! That happens to everyone," remarked Kuvalda; "but go on with your lies."

"She was thin, but she ate a lot, and even died from over-eating."

"You poisoned her, you hunchback!" said Abyedok, confidently.

"No, by God! It was from eating sturgeon," said Paltara Taras.

"But I say that you poisoned her!" declared Abyedok, decisively. It often happened, that having said something absolutely impossible and without proof, he kept on repeating it, beginning in a childish, capricious tone, and gradually raising his voice to a mad shriek.

The Deacon stood up for his friend. "No; he did not poison her. He had no reason to do so."

"But I say that he poisoned her!" swore Abyedok.

"Silence!" shouted the Captain, threateningly, becoming still angrier. He looked at his friends with his blinking eyes, and not discovering anything to further provoke his rage in their half-tipsy faces, he lowered his head, sat still for a little while, and then turned over on his back on the ground. Meteor was biting cucumbers. He took a cucumber in his hand without looking at it, put nearly half of it into his mouth, and bit it with his yellow teeth, so that the juice spurted out in all directions and ran over his cheeks. He did not seem to want to eat, but this process pleased him. Martyanoff sat motionless on the ground, like a statue, and looked in a dull manner at the half-vedro bottle, already getting empty. Abyedok lay on his belly and coughed, shaking all over his small body. The rest of the dark, silent figures sat and lay around in all sorts of positions, and their tatters made them look like untidy animals, created by some strange, uncouth deity to make a mockery of man.

"There once lived a lady in Suzdale,
  A strange lady,
 She fell into hysterics,
  Most unpleasantly!"

sang the Deacon in low tones embracing Aleksei Maksimovitch, who was smiling kindly into his face.

Paltaras Taras giggled voluptuously.

The night was approaching. High up in the sky the
stars were shining . . . and on the mountain and in
the town the lights of the lamps were appearing. The
whistles of the steamers were heard all over the river,
and the doors of Vaviloff's eating-house opened noisily.
Two dark figures entered the courtyard, and one of
them asked in a hoarse voice:

"Are you drinking?" And the other said in a jealous
aside:

"Just see what devils they are!"

Then a hand stretched over the Deacon's head and
took away the bottle, and the characteristic sound of
vodki being poured into a glass was heard. Then they
all protested loudly.

"Oh this is sad!" shouted the Deacon. "Krivoi, let
us remember the ancients! Let us sing 'On the Banks
of Babylonian Rivers.'"

"But can he?" asked Simtsoff.

"He? He was a chorister in the Bishop's choir. Now
then, Krivoi! . . . On the r-i-v-e-r-s——" The Deacon's voice was loud and hoarse and cracked, but his
friend sang in a shrill falsetto.

The dirty building loomed large in the darkness and
seemed to be coming nearer, threatening the singers,
who were arousing its dull echoes. The heavy, pompous clouds were floating in the sky over their heads.
One of the "creatures that once were men" was snoring;
while the rest of them, not yet so drunk as he was, ate

and drank quietly or spoke to each other at long intervals.

It was unusual for them to be in such low spirits during such a feast, with so much vodki. Somehow the drink tonight did not seem to have its usual exhilarating effect.

"Stop howling, you dogs!" . . . said the Captain to the singers, raising his head from the ground to listen. "Some one is passing . . . in a droshky. . . ."

A droshky at such a time in the main street could not but attract general attention. Who would risk crossing the ditches between it and the town, and why? They all raised their heads and listened. In the silence of the night the wheels were distinctly heard. They came gradually nearer. A voice was heard, asking roughly:

"Well, where then?"

Someone answered, "It must be there, that house."

"I shall not go any farther."

"They are coming here!" shouted the Captain.

"The police!" someone whispered in great alarm.

"In a droshky! Fool!" said Martyanoff, quietly.

Kuvalda got up and went to the entrance.

"Is this a lodging-house?" asked someone, in a trembling voice.

"Yes. Belonging to Aristid Kuvalda . . ." said the Captain, roughly.

"Oh! Did a reporter, one Titoff, live here?"

"Aha! Have you brought him?"

"Yes . . ."

"Drunk?"

"Ill."

"That means he is very drunk. Ay, teacher! Now, then, get up!"

"Wait, I will help you . . . He is very ill . . . he has been with me for the last two days . . . Take him under the arms . . . The doctor has seen him. He is very bad."

Tyapa got up and walked to the entrance, but Abye-dok laughed, and took another drink.

"Strike a light, there!" shouted the Captain.

Meteor went into the house and lighted the lamp. Then a thin line of light streamed out over the court-yard, and the Captain and another man managed to get the teacher into the dosshouse. His head was hanging on his breast, his feet trailed on the ground, and his arms hung limply as if broken. With Tyapa's help they placed him on a wide board. He was shivering all over.

"We worked on the same paper . . . he is very un-lucky. ` . . . I said, 'Stay in my house, you are not in the way,' . . . but he begged me to send him 'home.' He was so excited about it that I brought him here, thinking it might do him good. . . . Home! This is it, isn't it?"

"Do you suppose he has a home anywhere else?" asked Kuvalda, roughly, looking at his friend. "Ty-apa, fetch me some cold water."

"I fancy I am of no more use," remarked the man in some confusion. The Captain looked at him critically. His clothes were rather shiny, and tightly buttoned up to his chin. His trousers were frayed, his hat almost yellow with age and crumpled like his lean and hungry face.

"No, you are not necessary! We have plenty like you here," said the Captain, turning away.

"Then, good-bye!" The man went to the door, and said quietly from there, "If anything happens . . . let me know in the publishing office. . . . My name is Rijoff. I might write a short obituary. . . . You see he was an active member of the Press."

"H'm, an obituary, you say? Twenty lines forty kopecks? I will do more than that. When he dies I will cut off one of his legs and send it to you. That will be much more profitable than an obituary. It will last you for three days. . . . His legs are fat. You devoured him when he was alive. You may as well continue to do so after he is dead . . ."

The man sniffed strangely and disappeared. The Captain sat down on the wooden board beside the teacher, felt his forehead and breast with his hands and called "Philip!"

The sound re-echoed from the dirty walls of the doss-house and died away.

"This is absurd, brother," said the Captain, quietly arranging the teacher's untidy hair with his hand. Then the Captain listened to his breathing, which was rapid and uneven, and looked at his sunken gray face. He sighed and looked upon him, knitting his eyebrows. The lamp was a bad one . . . The light was fitful, and dark shadows flickered on the dosshouse walls. The Captain watched them, scratching his beard.

Tyapa returned, bringing a vedro of water, and plac-- ing it beside the teacher's head, he took his arm as if to raise him up.

"The water is not necessary," and the Captain shook his head.

"But we must try to revive him," said the old rag-collector.

"Nothing is needed," said the Captain, decidedly.

They sat silently looking at the teacher.

"Let us go and drink, old devil!"

"But he?"

"Can you do him any good?"

Tyapa turned his back on the teacher, and both went out into the courtyard to their companions.

"What is it?" asked Abyedok, turning his sharp nose to the old man.

The snoring of those who were asleep, and the tinkling sound of pouring vodki was heard. . . . The Deacon was murmuring something. The clouds swam low, so low that it seemed as if they would touch the roof of the house and would knock it over on the group of men.

"Ah! One feels sad when someone near at hand is dying," faltered the Captain, with his head down. No one answered him.

"He was the best among you . . . the cleverest, the most respectable . . . I mourn for him."

"R-e-s-t with the Saints. . . . Sing, you crooked hunchback!" roared the Deacon, digging his friend in the ribs.

"Be quiet!" shouted Abyedok, jumping vengefully to his feet.

"I will give him one on the head," proposed Martyanoff, raising his head from the ground.

"You are not asleep?" Aristid Fomich asked him very softly. "Have you heard about our teacher?"

Martyanoff lazily got up from the ground, looked at the line of light coming out of the dosshouse, shook his head and silently sat down beside the Captain.

"Nothing particular . . . The man is dying . . ." remarked the Captain, shortly.

"Have they been beating him?" asked Abyedok, with great interest. The Captain gave no answer. He was drinking vodki at the moment. "They must have known we had something in which to commemorate him after his death!" continued Abyedok, lighting a cigarette. Someone laughed, someone sighed. Generally speaking, the conversation of Abyedok and the Captain did not interest them, and they hated having to think at all. They had always felt the teacher to be an uncommon man, but now many of them were drunk and the others sad and silent. Only the Deacon suddenly drew himself up straight and howled wildly:

"And may the righteous r—e—s—t!"

"You idiot!" hissed Abyedok. "What are you howling for?"

"Fool!" said Tyapa's hoarse voice. "When a man is dying one must be quiet . . . so that he may have peace."

Silence reigned once more. The cloudy sky threatened thunder, and the earth was covered with the thick darkness of an autumn night.

"Let us go on drinking!" proposed Kuvalda, filling up the glasses.

"I will go and see if he wants anything," said Tyapa.

"He wants a coffin!" jeered the Captain.

"Don't speak about that," begged Abyedok in a low voice.

Meteor rose and followed Tyapa. The Deacon tried to get up, but fell and swore loudly.

When Tyapa had gone the Captain touched Martyanoff's shoulder and said in low tones:

"Well, Martyanoff . . . You must feel it more than the others. You were . . . But let that go to the Devil . . . Don't you pity Philip?"

"No," said the ex-jailer, quietly, "I do not feel things of this sort, brother . . . I have learned better . . . this life is disgusting after all. I speak seriously when I say that I should like to kill someone."

"Do you?" said the Captain, indistinctly. "Well . . . let's have another drink . . . It's not a long job ours, a little drink and then . . ."

The others began to wake up, and Simtsoff shouted in a blissful voice: "Brothers! One of you pour out a glass for the old man!"

They poured out a glass and gave it to him. Having drunk it he tumbled down again, knocking against another man as he fell. Two or three minutes' silence ensued, dark as the autumn night.

"What do you say?"

"I say that he was a good man . . . a quiet and good man," whispered a low voice.

"Yes, and he had money, too . . . and he never refused it to a friend . . ."

Again silence ensued.

"He is dying!" said Tyapa, hoarsely, from behind the

Captain's head. Aristid Fomich got up, and went with firm steps into the dosshouse.

"Don't go!" Tyapa stopped him. "Don't go! You are drunk! It is not right." The Captain stopped and thought.

"And what is right on this earth? Go to the Devil!" And he pushed Tyapa aside.

On the walls of the dosshouse the shadows were creeping, seeming to chase each other. The teacher lay on the board at full length and snored. His eyes were wide open, his naked breast rose and fell heavily, the corners of his mouth foamed, and on his face was an expression as if he wished to say something very important, but found it difficult to do so. The Captain stood with his hands behind him, and looked at him in silence. He then began in a silly way:

"Philip! Say something to me . . . a word of comfort to a friend . . . come. . . . I love you, brother! . . . All men are beasts. . . . You were the only man for me . . . though you were a drunkard. Ah! how you did drink vodki, Philip! That was the ruin of you! You ought to have listened to me, and controlled yourself. . . . Did I not once say to you . . . ?"

The mysterious, all-destroying reaper, called Death, made up his mind to finish the terrible work quickly, as if insulted by the presence of this drunken man at the dark and solemn struggle. The teacher sighed deeply, and quivered all over, stretched himself out, and died. The Captain stood shaking to and fro, and continued to talk to him.

"Do you want me to bring you vodki? But it is better

that you should not drink, Philip . . . control yourself or else drink! Why should you really control yourself? For what reason, Philip? For what reason?"

He took him by the foot and drew him closer to himself.

"Are you dozing, Philip? Well, then, sleep . . . Good-night. . . . To-morrow I shall explain all this to you, and you will understand that it is not really necessary to deny yourself anything. . . . But go on sleeping now . . . if you are not dead."

He went out to his friends, followed by the deep silence, and informed them:

"Whether he is sleeping or dead, I do not know . . . I am a little drunk."

Tyapa bent further forward than usual and crossed himself respectfully. Martyanoff dropped to the ground and lay there. Abyedok moved quietly, and said in a low and wicked tone:

"May you all go to the Devil! Dead? What of that? Why should I care? Why should I speak about it? It will be time enough when I come to die myself. . . . I am not worse than other people."

"That is true," said the Captain, loudly, and fell to the ground. "The time will come when we shall all die like others. . . . Ha! ha! How shall we live? . . . That is nothing. . . . But we shall die like everyone else, and this is the whole end of life, take my word for it. A man lives only to die, and he dies . . . and if this be so what does it matter how or where he died or how he lived? Am I right, Martyanoff? Let us therefore drink . . . while we still have life!"

The rain began to fall. Thick, close darkness covered the figures that lay scattered over the ground, half drunk, half asleep. The light in the windows of the dosshouse flickered, paled, and suddenly disappeared. Probably the wind blew it out or else the oil was exhausted. The drops of rain sounded strangely on the iron roof of the dosshouse. Above the mountain where the town lay the ringing of bells was heard, rung by the watchers in the churches. The brazen sound coming from the belfry rang out into the dark and died away, and before its last indistinct note was drowned another stroke was heard and the monotonous silence was again broken by the melancholy clang of bells.

*　　*　　*　　*　　*

The next morning Tyapa was the first to wake up. Lying on his back he looked up into the sky. Only in such a position did his deformed neck permit him to see the clouds above his head.

This morning the sky was of a uniform gray. Up there hung the damp, cold mist of dawn, almost extinguishing the sun, hiding the unknown vastness behind and pouring despondency over the earth. Tyapa crossed himself, and leaning on his elbow, looked round to see whether there was any vodki left. The bottle was there, but it was empty. Crossing over his companions he looked into the glasses.from which they had drunk, found one of them almost full, emptied it, wiped his lips with his sleeve, and began to shake the Captain.

The Captain raised his head and looked at him with sad eyes.

"We must inform the police . . .   Get up!"

"Of what?" asked the Captain, sleepily and angrily.

"What, is he not dead?" . . .

"Who?"

"The learned one." . . .

"Philip? Ye-es!"

"Did you forget? . . . Alas!" said Tyapa, hoarsely.
The Captain rose to his feet, yawned and stretched himself till all his bones cracked.

"Well, then! Go and give information. . . ."

"I will not go . . . I do not like them," said the
Captain morosely.

"Well, then, wake up the Deacon . . . I shall go,
at any rate."

"All right! . . . Deacon, get up!"

The Captain entered the dosshouse, and stood at the
teacher's feet. The dead man lay at full length, his left
hand on his breast, the right hand held as if ready to
strike some one.

The Captain thought that if the teacher got up now,
he would be as tall as Paltara Taras. Then he sat by
the side of the dead man and sighed, as he remembered
that they had lived together for the last three years.
Tyapa entered holding his head like a goat which is
ready tc butt.

He sat down quietly and seriously on the opposite side
of the teacher's body, looked into the dark, silent face,
and began to sob.

"So . . . he is dead . . . I too shall die soon . . ."

"It is quite time for that!" said the Captain,
gloomily.

"It is," Tyapa agreed. "You ought to die too. . . . Anything is better than this. . . . "

"But perhaps death might be worse? How do you know?"

"It could not be worse. When you die you have only God to deal with . . . but here you have to deal with men . . . and men—what are they?"

"Enough! . . . Be quiet!" interrupted Kuvalda, angrily.

And in the dawn, which filled the dosshouse, a solemn stillness reigned over all. Long and silently they sat at the feet of their dead companion, seldom looking at him, and both plunged in thought. Then Tyapa asked:

"Will you bury him?"

"I? No, let the police bury him!"

"You took money from Vaviloff for this petition . . . and I will give you some if you have not enough." . . .

"Though I have his money . . . still I shall not bury him."

"That is not right. You are robbing the dead. I will tell them all that you want to keep his money." . . . Tyapa threatened him.

"You are a fool, you old devil!" said Kuvalda, contemptuously.

"I am not a fool . . . but it is not right nor friendly."

"Enough! Be off!"

"How much money is there?"

"Twenty-five roubles," . . . said Kuvalda, absently.

"So! . . . You might gain a five-rouble note." . . .

"You old scoundrel! . . ." And looking into Tyapa's face the Captain swore.

"Well, what? Give . . ."

"Go to the Devil! . . . I am going to spend this money in erecting a monument to him."

"What does he want that for?"

"I will buy a stone and an anchor. I shall place the stone on the grass, and attach the anchor to it with a very heavy chain."

"Why? You are playing tricks . . ."

"Well . . . It is no business of yours."

"Look out! I shall tell . . ." again threatened Tyapa.

Aristid Fomich looked at him sullenly and said nothing. Again they sat there in that silence which, in the presence of the dead, is so full of mystery.

"Listen . . . They are coming!" Tyapa got up and went out of the dosshouse.

Then there appeared at the door the Doctor, the Police Inspector of the district, and the examining Magistrate or Coroner. All three came in turn, looked at the dead teacher, and then went out, throwing suspicious glances at Kuvalda. He sat there, without taking any notice of them, until the Police Inspector asked him:

"Of what did he die?"

"Ask him . . . I think his evil life hastened his end."

"What?" asked the Coroner.

"I say that he died of a disease to which he had not been accustomed . . ."

"H'm, yes. Had he been ill long?"

"Bring him over here, I cannot see him properly," said the Doctor, in a melancholy tone. "Probably there are signs of . . ."

"Now, then, ask someone here to carry him out!" the Police Inspector ordered Kuvalda.

"Go and ask them yourself! He is not in my way here . . . " the Captain replied, indifferently.

"Well!" . . . shouted the Inspector, making a ferocious face.

"Phew!" answered Kuvalda, without moving from his place and gnashing his teeth restlessly.

"The Devil take it!" shouted the Inspector, so madly that the blood rushed to his face. "I'll make you pay for this! I'll——"

"Good-morning, gentlemen!" said the merchant Petunikoff, with a sweet smile, making his appearance in the doorway.

He looked round, trembled, took off his cap and crossed himself. Then a pompous, wicked smile crossed his face, and, looking at the Captain, he inquired respectfully:

"What has happened? Has there been a murder here?"

"Yes, something of that sort," replied the Coroner.

Petunikoff sighed deeply, crossed himself again, and spoke in an angry tone.

"By God! It is just as I feared. It always ends in your having to come here. . . . Ay, ay, ay! God save everyone. Times without number have I refused to lease this house to this man, and he has always won

me over, and I was afraid. You know. . . . They are
such awful people . . . better give it them, I thought,
or else . . ."

He covered his face with his hands, tugged at his
beard, and sighed again.

"They are very dangerous men, and this man here is
their leader . . . the attaman of the robbers."

"But we will make him smart!" promised the Inspector, looking at the Captain with revengeful eyes.

"Yes, brother, we are old friends of yours . . ." said
Kuvalda in a familiar tone. "How many times have I
paid you to be quiet?"

"Gentlemen!" shouted the Inspector, "did you hear
him? I want you to bear witness to this. Aha, I shall
make short work of you, my friend, remember!"

"Don't count your chickens before they are hatched
. . . my friend," said Aristid Fomich.

The Doctor, a young man with eye-glasses, looked at
him curiously, the Coroner with an attention that boded
him no good, Petunikoff with triumph, while the Inspector could hardly restrain himself from throwing
himself upon him.

The dark figure of Martyanoff appeared at the door
of the dosshouse. He entered quietly, and stood behind Petunikoff, so that his chin was on a level with
the merchant's head. Behind him stood the Deacon,
opening his small, swollen, red eyes.

"Let us be doing something, gentlemen," suggested
the Doctor. Martyanoff made an awful grimace, and
suddenly sneezed on Petunikoff's head. The latter gave
a yell, sat down hurriedly, and then jumped aside, al-

most knocking down the Inspector, into whose open arms he fell.

"Do you see," said the frightened merchant, pointing to Martyanoff, "do you see what kind of men they are."

Kuvalda burst out laughing. The Doctor and the Coroner smiled too, and at the door of the dosshouse the group of figures was increasing . . . sleepy figures, with swollen faces, red, inflamed eyes, and dishevelled hair, staring rudely at the Doctor, the Coroner, and the Inspector.

"Where are you going?" said the policeman on guard at the door, catching hold of their tatters and pushing them aside. But he was one against many, and, without taking any notice, they all entered and stood there, reeking of vodki, silent and evil-looking.

Kuvalda glanced at them, then at the authorities, who were angry at the intrusion of these ragamuffins, and said, smilingly, "Gentlemen, perhaps you would like to make the acquaintance of my lodgers and friends? Would you? But, whether you wish it or not, you will have to make their acquaintance sooner or later in the course of your duties."

The Doctor smiled in an embarrassed way. The Coroner pressed his lips together, and the Inspector saw that it was time to go. Therefore, he shouted:

"Sideroff! Whistle! Tell them to bring a cart here."

"I will go," said Petunikoff, coming forward from a corner. "You had better take it away to-day, sir, I want to. pull down this hole. Go away! or else I shall apply to the police!"

The policeman's whistle echoed through the court-yard. At the door of the dosshouse its inhabitants stood in a group, yawning, and scratching themselves.

"And so you do not wish to be introduced? That is rude of you!" laughed Aristid Fomich.

Petunikoff took his purse from his pocket, took out two five-kopeck pieces, put them at the feet of the dead man, and crossed himself.

"God have mercy . . . on the burial of the sin-ful . . ."

"What!" yelled the Captain, "you give for the burial? Take them away, I say, you scoundrel! How dare you give your stolen kopecks for the burial of an honest man? I will tear you limb from limb!"

"Your Honor!" cried the terrified merchant to the Inspector, seizing him by the elbow.

The Doctor and the Coroner jumped aside. The Inspector shouted:

"Sideroff, come here!"

"The creatures that once were men" stood along the wall, looking and listening with an interest, which put new life into their broken-down bodies.

Kuvalda, shaking his fist at Petunikoff's head, roared and rolled his eyes like a wild beast.

"Scoundrel and thief! Take back your money! Dirty worm! Take it back, I say . . . or else I shall cram it down your throat. . . . Take your five-kopeck pieces!"

Petunikoff put out his trembling hand toward his mite, and protecting his head from Kuvalda's fist with the other hand, said:

"You are my witnesses, Sir Inspector, and you good people!"

"We are not good people, merchant!" said the voice of Abyedok, trembling with anger.

The Inspector whistled impatiently, with his other hand protecting Petunikoff, who was stooping in front of him as if trying to enter his belly.

"You dirty toad! I shall compel you to kiss the feet of the dead man. How would you like that?" And catching Petunikoff by the neck, Kuvalda hurled him against the door, as if he had been a cat.

The "creatures that once were men" sprang aside quickly to let the merchant fall. And down he fell at their feet, crying wildly:

"Murder! Help! Murder!"

Martyanoff slowly raised his foot, and brought it down heavily on the merchant's head. Abyedok spat in his face with a grin. The merchant, creeping on all-fours, threw himself into the courtyard, at which everyone laughed. But by this time the two policemen had arrived, and pointing to Kuvalda, the Inspector said, pompously:

"Arrest him, and bind him hand and foot!"

"You dare not! . . . I shall not run away . . . I will go wherever you wish, . . ." said Kuvalda, freeing himself from the policemen at his side.

The "creatures that once were men" disappeared one after the other. A cart entered the yard. Some ragged wretches brought out the dead man's body.

"I'll teach you! You just wait!" thundered the Inspector at Kuvalda.

"How now, ataman?" asked Petunikoff maliciously, excited and pleased at the sight of his enemy in bonds. "What, you fell into the trap? Eh? You just wait . . ."

But Kuvalda was quiet now. He stood strangely straight and silent between the two policemen, watching the teacher's body being placed in the cart. The man who was holding the head of the corpse was very short, and could not manage to place it on the cart at the same time as the legs. For a moment the body hung as if it would fall to the ground, and hide itself beneath the earth, away from these foolish and wicked disturbers of its peace.

"Take him away!" ordered the Inspector, pointing to the Captain.

Kuvalda silently moved forward without protestation, passing the cart on which was the teacher's body. He bowed his head before it without looking. Martyanoff, with his strong face, followed him. The courtyard of the merchant Petunikoff emptied quickly.

"Now then, go on!" called the driver, striking the horses with the whip. The cart moved off over the rough surface of the courtyard. The teacher was covered with a heap of rags, and his belly projected from beneath them. It seemed as if he were laughing quietly at the prospect of leaving the dosshouse, never, never to return. Petunikoff, who was following him with his eyes, crossed himself, and then began to shake the dust and rubbish off his clothes, and the more he shook himself the more pleased and self-satisfied did he feel. He saw the tall figure of Aristid Fomich Kuvalda, in a gray cap with a red band, with his arms bound behind his back, being led away.

Petunikoff smiled the smile of the conqueror, and went back into the dosshouse, but suddenly he stopped and trembled. At the door facing him stood an old man with a stick in his hand and a large bag on his back, a horrible old man in rags and tatters, which covered his bony figure. He bent under the weight of his burden, and lowered his head on his breast, as if he wished to attack the merchant.

"What are you? Who are you?" shouted Petunikoff.

"A man . . ." he answered in a hoarse voice. This hoarseness pleased and tranquillized Petunikoff, he even smiled.

"A man! And are there really men like you?" Stepping aside he let the old man pass. He went, saying slowly:

"Men are of various kinds . . . as God wills. . . . There are worse than me . . . still worse . . . Yes . . ."

The cloudy sky hung silently over the dirty yard and over the cleanly-dressed man with the pointed beard, who was walking about there, measuring distances with his steps and with his sharp eyes. On the roof of the old house a crow perched and croaked, thrusting its head now backward, now forward. In the lowering gray clouds, which hid the sky, there was something hard and merciless, as if they had gathered together to wash all the dirt off the face of this unfortunate, suffering, and sorrowful earth.

TWENTY-SIX MEN AND A GIRL

THERE were six-and-twenty of us—six-and-twenty living machines in a damp, underground cellar, where from morning till night we kneaded dough and rolled it into kringels. Opposite the underground window of our cellar was a bricked area, green and mouldy with moisture. The window was protected from outside with a close iron grating, and the light of the sun could not pierce through the window panes, covered as they were with flour dust.

Our employer had bars placed in front of the windows, so that we should not be able to give a bit of his bread to passing beggars, or to any of our fellows who were out of work and hungry. Our employer called us rogues, and gave us half-rotten tripe to eat for our mid-day meal, instead of meat. It was swelteringly close for us cooped up in that stone underground chamber, under the low, heavy, soot-blackened, cobwebby ceiling. Dreary and sickening was our life between its thick, dirty, mouldy walls.

Unrefreshed, and with a feeling of not having had our sleep out, we used to get up at five o'clock in the morning; and before six, we were already seated, worn out and apathetic, at the table, rolling out the dough which our mates had already prepared while we slept. The whole day, from ten in the early morning until ten at night, some of us sat round that table, working up in our hands the yielding paste, rolling it to and fro so that it should not get stiff; while the others kneaded the swelling mass of dough. And the whole day the simmering water in the kettle, where the kringels were being cooked, sang low and sadly; and the baker's shovel scraped harshly over the oven floor, as he threw the slippery bits of dough out of the kettle on the heated bricks.

From morning till evening wood was burning in the oven, and the red glow of the fire gleamed and flickered over the walls of the bake-shop, as if silently mocking us. The giant oven was like the misshapen head of a monster in a fairy tale; it thrust itself up out of the floor, opened wide jaws, full of glowing fire, and blew hot breath upon us; it seemed to be ever watching out of its black air-holes our interminable work. Those two deep holes were like eyes—the cold, pitiless eyes of a monster. They watched us always with the same darkened glance, as if they were weary of seeing before them such eternal slaves, from whom they could expect nothing human, and therefore scorned them with the cold scorn of wisdom.

In meal dust, in the mud which we brought in from the yard on our boots, in the hot, sticky atmosphere, day in, day out, we rolled the dough into kringels, which we moistened with our own sweat. And we hated our work with a glowing hatred; we never ate what had passed through our hands, and preferred black bread to

kringels. Sitting opposite each other, at a long table—
nine facing nine—we moved our hands and fingers mechanically during endlessly long hours, till we were so
accustomed to our monotonous work that we ceased to
pay any attention to it.

We had all studied each other so constantly, that each
of us knew every wrinkle of his mates' faces. It was
not long also before we had exhausted almost every
topic of conversation; that is why we were most of the
time silent, unless we were chaffing each other; but one
cannot always find something about which to chaff another man, especially when that man is one's mate.
Neither were we much given to finding fault with one
another; how, indeed, could one of us poor devils be in
a position to find fault with another, when we were all
of us half dead and, as it were, turned to stone? For
the heavy drudgery seemed to crush all feeling out of
us. But silence is only terrible and fearful for those
who have said everything and have nothing more to say
to each other; for men, on the contrary, who have never
begun to communicate with one another, it is easy and
simple.

Sometimes, too, we sang; and this is how it happened
that we began to sing: one of us would sigh deeply
in the midst of our toil, like an overdriven horse, and
then we would begin one of those songs whose gentle
swaying melody seems always to ease the burden on
the singer's heart.

At first one sang by himself, and we others sat in
silence listening to his solitary song, which, under the
heavy vaulted roof of the cellar, died gradually away,

and became extinguished, like a little fire in the steppes, on a wet autumn night, when the gray heaven hangs like a heavy mass over the earth. Then another would join in with the singer, and now two soft, sad voices would break into song in our narrow, dull hole of a cellar. Suddenly others would join in, and the song would roll forward like a wave, would grow louder and swell upward, till it would seem as if the damp, foul walls of our stone prison were widening out and opening. Then, all six-and-twenty of us would be singing; our loud, harmonious song would fill the whole cellar, our voices would travel outside and beyond, striking, as it were, against the walls in moaning sobs and sighs, moving our hearts with soft, tantalizing ache, tearing open old wounds, and awakening longings.

The singers would sigh deeply and heavily; suddenly one would become silent and listen to the others singing, then let his voice flow once more in the common tide. Another would exclaim in a stifled voice, "Ah!" and would shut his eyes, while the deep, full sound waves would show him, as it were, a road, in front of him—a sunlit, broad road in the distance, which he himself, in thought, wandered along.

But the flame flickers once more in the huge oven, the baker scrapes incessantly with his shovel, the water simmers in the kettle, and the flicker of the fire on the wall dances as before in silent mockery. While in other men's words we sing out our dumb grief, the weary burden of live men robbed of the sunlight, the burden of slaves.

So we lived, we six-and-twenty, in the vault-like cellar of a great stone house, and we suffered each one of us, as if we had to bear on our shoulders the whole three storys of that house.

But we had something else good, besides the singing —something we loved, that perhaps took the place of the sunshine.

In the second story of our house there was established a gold-embroiderer's shop, and there, living among the other embroidery girls, was Tanya, a little maid-servant of sixteen. Every morning there peeped in through the glass door a rosy little face, with merry blue eyes; while a ringing, tender voice called out to us:

"Little prisoners! Have you any kringels, please, for me?"

At that clear sound, we knew so well, we all used to turn round, gazing with simple-hearted joy at the pure girlish face which smiled at us so sweetly. The sight of the small nose pressed against the window-pane, and of the white teeth gleaming between the half-open lips, had become for us a daily pleasure. Tumbling over each other we used to jump up to open the door, and she would step in, bright and cheerful, holding out her apron, with her head thrown on one side, and a smile on her lips. Her thick, long chestnut hair fell over her shoulder and across her breast. But we, ugly, dirty and misshapen as we were, looked up at her—the threshold door was four steps above the floor—looked up at her with heads thrown back, wishing her good-morning, and speaking strange, unaccustomed words, which we kept

for her only. Our voices became softer when we spoke
to her, our jests were lighter. For her—everything was
different with us. The baker took from his oven a
shovel of the best and the brownest kringels, and threw
them deftly into Tanya's apron.

"Be off with you now, or the boss will catch you!" we
warned her each time. She laughed roguishly, called out
cheerfully: "Good-bye, poor prisoners!" and slipped
away as quick as a mouse.

That was all. But long after she had gone we talked
about her to one another with pleasure. It was always
the same thing as we had said yesterday and the day
before, because everything about us, including ourselves
and her, remained the same—as yesterday—and as
always.

Painful and terrible it is when a man goes on living,
while nothing changes around him; and when such an
existence does not finally kill his soul, then the monotony becomes with time, even more and more painful.
Generally we spoke about women in such a way, that
sometimes it was loathsome to us ourselves to hear our
rude, shameless talk. The women whom we knew de-
served perhaps nothing better. But about Tanya we
never let fall an evil word; none of us ever ventured
so much as to lay a hand on her, even too free a jest
she never heard from us. Maybe this was so because
she never remained for long with us; she flashed on our
eyes like a star falling from the sky, and vanished; and
maybe because she was little and very beautiful, and
everything beautiful calls forth respect, even in coarse
people. And besides—though our life of penal labor had

made us dull beasts, oxen, we were still men, and, like all men, could not live without worshipping something or other. Better than her we had none, and none but her took any notice of us, living in the cellar—no one, though there were dozens of people in the house. And then, too—most likely, this was the chief thing—we all regarded her as something of our own, something existing as it were only by virtue of our kringels. We took on ourselves in turns the duty of providing her with hot kringels, and this became for us like a daily sacrifice to our idol, it became almost a sacred rite, and every day it bound us more closely to her. Besides kringels, we gave Tanya a great deal of advice—to wear warmer clothes, not to run upstairs too quickly, not to carry heavy bundles of wood. She listened to all our counsels with a smile, answered them by a laugh, and never took our advice, but we were not offended at that; all we wanted was to show how much care we bestowed upon her.

Often she would apply to us with different requests, she asked us, for instance, to open the heavy door into the store-cellar, and to chop wood: with delight and a sort of pride, we did this for her, and everything else she wanted.

But when one of us asked her to mend his solitary shirt for him, she said, with a laugh of contempt:

"What next! A likely idea!"

We made great fun of the queer fellow who could entertain such an idea, and—never asked her to do anything else. We loved her—all is said in that. Man always wants to lay his love on someone, though sometimes he crushes, sometimes he sullies, with it; he may poison another life because he loves without respecting the beloved. We were bound to love Tanya, for we had no one else to love.

At times one of us would suddenly begin to reason like this:

"And why do we make so much of the wench? What is there in her? eh? What a to-do we make about her!"

The man who dared to utter such words we promptly and coarsely cut short—we wanted something to love: we had found it and loved it, and what we twenty-six loved must be for each of us unalterable, as a holy thing, and anyone who acted against us in this was our enemy. We loved, maybe, not what was really good, but you see there were twenty-six of us, and so we always wanted to see what was precious to us held sacred by the rest.

Our love is not less burdensome than hate, and maybe that is just why some proud souls maintain that our hate is more flattering than our love. But why do they not run away from us, if it is so?

* * * * *

Besides our department, our employer had also a bread-bakery; it was in the same house, separated from our hole only by a wall; but the bakers—there were four of them—held aloof from us, considering their work superior to ours, and therefore themselves better than us; they never used to come into our workroom, and laughed contemptuously at us when they met us in the yard. We, too, did not go to see them; this was forbidden by our employer, from fear that we should steal the fancy bread. We did not like the bakers, because we envied them; their work was lighter than ours, they were paid more, and were better fed; they had a light, spacious workroom, and they were all so clean and healthy—and that made them hateful to us. We all looked gray and yellow; three of us had syphilis, several suffered from skin diseases, one was completely crippled by rheumatism. On holidays and in their leisure time the bakers wore pea-jackets and creaking boots, two of them had accordions, and they all used to go for strolls in the town gardens—we wore filthy rags and leather clogs or plaited shoes on our feet, the police would not let us into the town gardens—could we possibly like the bakers?

And one day we learned that their chief baker had been drunk, the master had sacked him and had already taken on another, and that this other was a soldier, wore a satin waistcoat and a watch and gold chain. We were inquisitive to get a sight of such a dandy, and in the hope of catching a glimpse of him we kept running one after another out into the yard.

But he came of his own accord into our room. Kicking at the door, he pushed it open, and leaving it ajar, stood in the doorway smiling, and said to us:

"God help the work! Good-morning, mates!"

The ice-cold air, which streamed in through the open door, curled in streaks of vapor round his feet. He stood on the threshold, looked us up and down, and under his fair, twisted mustache gleamed big yellow teeth. His waistcoat was really something quite out of the common, blue-flowered, brilliant with shining little buttons of red stones. He also wore a watch chain.

He was a fine fellow, this soldier; tall, healthy, rosy-cheeked, and his big, clear eyes had a friendly, cheerful glance. He wore on his head a white starched cap, and from under his spotlessly clean apron peeped the pointed toes of fashionable, well-blacked boots.

Our baker asked him politely to shut the door. The soldier did so without hurrying himself, and began to question us about the master. We explained to him, all speaking together, that our employer was a thorough-going brute, a rogue, a knave, and a slave-driver; in a word, we repeated to him all that can and must be said about an employer, but cannot be repeated here. The soldier listened to us, twisted his mustache, and watched us with a friendly, open-hearted look.

"But haven't you got a lot of girls here?" he asked suddenly.

Some of us began to laugh deferentially, others put on a meaning expression, and one of us explained to the soldier that there were nine girls here.

"You make the most of them?" asked the soldier, with a wink.

We laughed, but not so loudly, and with some em-barrassment. Many of us would have liked to have shown the soldier that we also were tremendous fellows with the girls, but not one of us could do so; and one of our number confessed as much, when he said in a low voice:

"That sort of thing is not in our line."

"Well, no; it wouldn't quite do for you," said the sol-

dier with conviction, after having looked us over.
"There is something wanting about you all. You don't
look the right sort. You've no sort of appearance; and
the women, you see, they like a bold appearance, they
will have a well set-up body. Everything has to be tip-
top for them. That's why they respect strength. They
want an arm like that!"

The soldier drew his right hand, with its turned-up
shirt sleeve, out of his pocket, and showed us his bare
arm. It was white and strong, and covered with shining yellow hairs.

"Leg and chest, all must be strong. And then a man
must be dressed in the latest fashion, so as to show off
his looks to advantage. Yes, all the women take to me.
Whether I call to them, or whether I beckon them, they
with one accord, five at a time, throw themselves at my
head."

He sat down on a flour sack, and told at length all
about the way women loved him, and how bold he was
with them. Then he left, and after the door had creaked
to behind him, we sat for a long time silent, and thought
about him and his talk. Then we all suddenly broke
silence together, and it became apparent that we were
all equally pleased with him. He was such a nice, open-
hearted fellow; he came to see us without any stand-
offishness, sat down and chatted. No one else came to
us like that, and no one else talked to us in that friendly
sort of way. And we continued to talk of him and his
coming triumph among the embroidery girls, who passed
us by with contemptuous sniffs when they saw us in
the yard, or who looked straight through us as if we

had been air. But we admired them always when we met them outside, or when they walked past our windows; in winter, in fur jackets and toques to match; in summer, in hats trimmed with flowers, and with colored parasols in their hands. We talked, however, about these girls in a way that would have made them mad with shame and rage, if they could have heard us.

"If only he does not get hold of little Tanya!" said the baker, suddenly, in an anxious tone of voice.

We were silent, for these words troubled us. Tanya had quite gone out of our minds, supplanted, put on one side by the strong, fine figure of the soldier.

Then began a lively discussion; some of us maintained that Tanya would never lower herself so; others thought she would not be able to resist him, and the third group proposed to give him a thrashing if he should try to annoy Tanya. And, finally, we all decided to watch the soldier and Tanya, and to warn the girl against him. This brought the discussion to an end.

Four weeks had passed by since then; during this time the soldier baked white bread, walked about with the gold-embroidery girls, visited us often, but did not talk any more about his conquests; only twisted his mustache, and licked his lips lasciviously.

Tanya called in as usual every morning for "little kringels," and was as gay and as nice and friendly with us as ever. We certainly tried once or twice to talk to her about the soldier, but she called him a "goggle-eyed calf," and made fun of him all round, and that set our minds at rest. We saw how the gold-embroidery girls carried on with the soldier, and we were proud of our girl; Tanya's behavior reflected honor on us all; we imitated her, and began in our talks to treat the soldier with small consideration. She became dearer to us, and we greeted her with more friendliness and kindliness every morning.

One day the soldier came to see us, a bit drunk, and sat down and began to laugh. When we asked him what he was laughing about, he explained to us:

"Why two of them—that Lydka girl and Grushka—have been clawing each other on my account. You should have seen the way they went for each other! Ha! ha! One got hold of the other one by the hair, threw her down on the floor of the passage, and sat on her! Ha! ha! ha! They scratched and tore each others' faces. It was enough to make one die with laughter! Why is it women can't fight fair? Why do they always scratch one another, eh?"

He sat on the bench, healthy, fresh and jolly; he sat there and went on laughing. We were silent. This time he made an unpleasant impression on us.

"Well, it's a funny thing what luck I have with the women-folk! Eh? I've laughed till I'm ill! One wink, and it's all over with them! It's the d-devil!"

He raised his white hairy hands, and slapped them down on his knees. And his eyes seem to reflect such frank astonishment, as if he were himself quite surprised at his good luck with women. His fat, red face glistened with delight and self satisfaction, and he licked his lips more than ever.

Our baker scraped the shovel violently and angrily along the oven floor, and all at once he said sarcastically:

"There's no great strength needed to pull up fir saplings, but try a real pine-tree."

"Why—what do you mean by saying that to me?" asked the soldier.

"Oh, well . . ."

"What is it?"

"Nothing—it slipped out!"

"No, wait a minute! What's the point? What pine-tree?"

Our baker did not answer, working rapidly away with the shovel at the oven; flinging into it the half-cooked kringels, taking out those that were done, and noisily throwing them on the floor to the boys who were stringing them on bast. He seemed to have forgotten the soldier and his conversation with him. But the soldier had all at once dropped into a sort of uneasiness. He got up on to his feet, and went to the oven, at the risk of knocking against the handle of the shovel, which was waving spasmodically in the air.

"No, tell me, do—who is it? You've insulted me. I? There's not one could withstand me, n-no! And you say such insulting things to me?"

He really seemed genuinely hurt. He must have had nothing else to pride himself on except his gift for seducing women; maybe, except for that, there was nothing living in him, and it was only that by which he could feel himself a living man.

There are men to whom the most precious and best thing in their lives appears to be some disease of their soul or body. They spend their whole life in relation to it, and only living by it, suffering from it, they sustain themselves on it, they complain of it to others, and so draw the attention of their fellows to themselves. For that they extract sympathy from people, and apart from it they have nothing at all. Take from them that disease, cure them, and they will be miserable, because they have lost their one resource in life—they are left empty then. Sometimes a man's life is so poor, that he is driven instinctively to prize his vice and to live by it; one may say for a fact that often men are vicious from boredom.

The soldier was offended, he went up to our baker and roared:

"No, tell me do—who?"

"Tell you?" the baker turned suddenly to him.

"Well?"

"You know Tanya?"

"Well?"

"Well, there then!   Only try."

"I?"

"You!"

"Her?   Why that's nothing to me—pooh!"

"We shall see!"

"You will see!   Ha! ha!"

"She'll——"

"Give me a month!"

"What a braggart you are, soldier!"

"A fortnight!   I'll prove it!   Who is it?   Tanya! Pooh!"

"Well, get out.   You're in my way!"

"A fortnight—and it's done!   Ah, you——"

"Get out, I say!"

Our baker, all at once, flew into a rage and brandished his shovel. The soldier staggered away from him in amazement, looked at us, paused, and softly, malignantly said, "Oh, all right, then!" and went away.

During the dispute we had all sat silent, absorbed in it. But when the soldier had gone, eager, loud talk and noise arose among us.

Some one shouted to the baker: "It's a bad job that you've started, Pavel!"

"Do your work!" answered the baker savagely.

We felt that the soldier had been deeply aggrieved, and that danger threatened Tanya. We felt this, and at the same time we were all possessed by a burning curiosity, most agreeable to us. What would happen? Would Tanya hold out against the soldier? And almost all cried confidently: "Tanya? She'll hold out! You won't catch her with your bare arms!"

We longed terribly to test the strength of our idol; we forcibly proved to each other that our divinity was a strong divinity and would come victorious out of this ordeal. We began at last to fancy that we had not worked enough on the soldier, that he would forget the dispute, and that we ought to pique his vanity more keenly. From that day we began to live a different life, a life of nervous tension, such as we had never known before. We spent whole days in arguing together; we all grew, as it were, sharper; and got to talk more and better. It seemed to us that we were playing some sort of game with the devil, and the stake on our side was Tanya. And when we learned from the bakers that the soldier had begun "running after our Tanya," we felt a sort of delighted terror, and life was so interesting that we did not even notice that our employer had taken advantage of our pre-occupation to increase our work by fourteen pounds of dough a day. We seemed, indeed, not even tired by our work. Tanya's name was on our lips all day long. And every day we looked for her with a certain special impatience. Sometimes we pictured to ourselves that she would come to us, and it would not be the same Tanya as of old, but somehow different. We said nothing to her, however, of the dispute regarding her. We asked her no questions, and behaved as well and affectionately to her as ever. But even in this a new element crept in, alien to our old feeling for Tanya—and that new element was keen curiosity, keen and cold as a steel knife.

"Mates! To-day the time's up!" our baker said to us one morning, as he set to work.

We were well aware of it without his reminder; but still we were thrilled.

"Look at her. She'll be here directly," suggested the baker.

One of us cried out in a troubled voice, "Why! as though one could notice anything!"

And again an eager, noisy discussion sprang up among us. To-day we were about to prove how pure and spotless was the vessel into which we had poured all that was best in us. This morning, for the first time, it became clear to us, that we really were playing a great game; that we might, indeed, through the exaction of this proof of purity, lose our divinity altogether.

During the whole of the intervening fortnight we had

heard that Tanya was persistently followed by the soldier, but not one of us had thought of asking her how she had behaved toward him. And she came every morning to fetch her kringels, and was the same toward us as ever.

This morning, too, we heard her voice outside: "You poor prisoners! Here I am!"

We opened the door, and when she came in we all remained, contrary to our usual custom, silent. Our eyes fixed on her, we did not know how to speak to her, what to ask her. And there we stood in front of her, a gloomy, silent crowd. She seemed to be surprised at this unusual reception; and suddenly we saw her turn white and become uneasy, then she asked, in a choking voice:

"Why are you—like this?"

"And you?" the baker flung at her grimly, never taking his eyes off her.

"What am I?"

"N—nothing."

"Well, then, give me quickly the little kringels."

Never before had she bidden us hurry.

"There's plenty of time," said the baker, not stirring, and not removing his eyes from her face.

Then, suddenly, she turned round and disappeared through the door.

The baker took his shovel and said, calmly turning away toward the oven:

"Well, that settles it! But a soldier! a common beast like that—a low cur!"

Like a flock of sheep we all pressed round the table,

sat down silently, and began listlessly to work. Soon, however, one of us remarked:

"Perhaps, after all——"

"Shut up!" shouted the baker.

We were all convinced that he was a man of judgment, a man who knew more than we did about things. And at the sound of his voice we were convinced of the soldier's victory, and our spirits became sad and downcast.

At twelve o'clock—while we were eating our dinners—the soldier came in. He was as clean and as smart as ever, and looked at us—as usual—straight in the eyes. But we were all awkward in looking at him.

"Now then, honored sirs, would you like me to show you a soldier's quality?" he said, chuckling proudly.

"Go out into the passage, and look through the crack—do you understand?"

We went into the passage, and stood all pushing against one another, squeezed up to the cracks of the wooden partition of the passage that looked into the yard. We had not to wait long. Very soon Tanya, with hurried footsteps and a careworn face, walked across the yard, jumping over the puddles of melting snow and mud: she disappeared into the store cellar. Then whistling, and not hurrying himself, the soldier followed in the same direction. His hands were thrust in his pockets; his mustaches were quivering.

Rain was falling, and we saw how its drops fell into the puddles, and the puddles were wrinkled by them. The day was damp and gray—a very dreary day. Snow still lay on the roofs, but on the ground dark patches of mud had begun to appear. And the snow on the roofs too was covered by a layer of brownish dirt. The rain fell slowly with a depressing sound. It was cold and disagreeable for us waiting.

The first to come out of the store cellar was the soldier; he walked slowly across the yard, his mustaches twitching, his hands in his pockets—the same as always.

Then—Tanya, too, came out. Her eyes—her eyes were radiant with joy and happiness, and her lips—were smiling. And she walked as though in a dream, staggering, with unsteady steps.

We could not bear this quietly. All of us at once rushed to the door, dashed out into the yard and—hissed at her, reviled her viciously, loudly, wildly.

She started at seeing us, and stood as though rooted in the mud under her feet. We formed a ring round her! and malignantly, without restraint, abused her with vile words, said shameful things to her.

We did this not loudly, not hurriedly, seeing that she could not get away, that she was hemmed in by us, and we could deride her to our hearts' content. I don't know why, but we did not beat her. She stood in the midst of us, and turned her head this way and that, as she heard our insults. And we—more and more violently flung at her the filth and venom of our words.

The color had left her face. Her blue eyes, so happy a moment before, opened wide, her bosom heaved, and her lips quivered.

We in a ring round her avenged ourselves on her as though she had robbed us. She belonged to us, we had lavished on her our best, and though that best was a beggar's crumb, still we were twenty-six, she was one, and so there was no pain we could give her equal to her guilt! How we insulted her! She was still mute, still gazed at us with wild eyes, and a shiver ran all over her.

We laughed, roared, yelled. Other people ran up from somewhere and joined us. One of us pulled Tanya by the sleeve of her blouse.

Suddenly her eyes flashed; deliberately she raised her hands to her head and straightening her hair she said loudly but calmly, straight in our faces:

"Ah, you miserable prisoners!"

And she walked straight at us, walked as directly as though we had not been before her, as though we were not blocking her way.

And hence it was that no one did actually prevent her passing.

Walking out of our ring, without turning round, she said loudly and with indescribable contempt:

"Ah, you scum—brutes."

And—was gone.

We were left in the middle of the yard, in the rain, under the gray sky without the sun.

Then we went mutely away to our damp stone cellar. As before—the sun never peeped in at our windows, and Tanya came no more!

CHELKASH

AN EPISODE

DARKENED by the dust of the dock, the blue southern sky is murky; the burning sun looks duskily into the greenish sea, as though through a thin gray veil. It can find no reflection in the water, continually cut up by the strokes of oars, the screws of steamers, the deep, sharp keels of Turkish feluccas and other sailing vessels, that pass in all directions, ploughing up the crowded harbor, where the free waves of the sea, pent up within granite walls, and crushed under the vast weights that glide over its crests, beat upon the sides of the ships and on the bank; beat and complain, churned up into foam and fouled with all sorts of refuse.

The jingle of the anchor chains, the rattle of the links of the trucks that bring down the cargoes, the metallic clank of sheets of iron falling on the stone pavement, the dull thud of wood, the creaking of the carts plying for hire, the whistles of the steamers, piercingly shrill and hoarsely roaring, the shouts of dock laborers, sailors, and customs officers—all these sounds melt into the deafening symphony of the working day, that hovering uncertainty hangs over the harbor, as though afraid to float upward and be lost. And

fresh waves of sound continually rise up from the earth
to join it; deep, grumbling, sullen reverberations setting
all around quaking; shrill, menacing notes that pierce
the ear and the dusty, sultry air.

The granite, the iron, the wood, the harbor pavement,
the ships and the men—all swelled the mighty strains
of this frenzied, impassioned hymn to Mercury. But
the voices of men, scarcely audible in it, were weak and
ludicrous. And the men, too, themselves, the first
source of all that uproar, were ludicrous and pitiable:
their little figures, dusty, tattered, nimble, bent under
the weight of goods that lay on their backs, under the
weight of cares that drove them hither and thither, in
the clouds of dust, in the sea of sweltering heat and din,
were so trivial and small in comparison with the colos-
sal iron monsters, the mountains of bales, the thundering railway trucks and all that they had created. Their
own creation had enslaved them, and stolen away their
individual life.

As they lay letting off steam, the heavy giant steamers whistled or hissed, or seemed to heave deep sighs,
and in every sound that came from them could be
heard the mocking note of ironical contempt for the
gray, dusty shapes of men, crawling about their decks
and filling their deep holds with the fruits of their
slavish toil. Ludicrous and pitiable were the long
strings of dock laborers bearing on their backs thousands
of tons of bread, and casting it into the iron bellies of
the ships to gain a few pounds of that same bread to
fill their own bellies—for their worse luck not made of
iron, but alive to the pangs of hunger. The men, tat-

tered, drenched with sweat, made dull by weariness, and din and heat; and the mighty machines, created by those men, shining, well-fed, serene, in the sunshine; machines which in the last resort are, after all, not set in motion by steam, but by the muscles and blood of their creators —in this contrast was a whole poem of cruel and frigid irony.

The clamor oppressed the spirit, the dust fretted the nostrils and blinded the eyes, the sweltering heat baked and exhausted the body, and everything—buildings, men, pavement—seemed strained, breaking, ready to burst, losing patience, on the verge of exploding into some immense catastrophe, some outbreak, after which one would be able to breathe freely and easily in the air refreshed by it. On the earth there would be quietness; and that dusty uproar, deafening, fretting the nerves, driving one to melancholy frenzy, would vanish; and in town, and sea and sky, it would be still and clear and pleasant. But that was only seeming. It seemed so because man has not yet grown weary of hoping for better things, and the longing to feel free is not dead in him.

Twelve times there rang out the regular musical peal of the bell. When the last brazen clang had died away, the savage orchestra of toil had already lost half its volume. A minute later it had passed into a dull, repining grumble. Now the voices of men and the splash of the sea could be heard more clearly. The dinner-hour had come.

CHAPTER I

WHEN the dock laborers, knocking off work, had scattered about the dock in noisy groups, buying various edibles from the women hawking food, and were settling themselves to dinner in shady corners on the pavement, there walked into their midst Grishka Chelkash, an old hunted wolf, well known to all the dock population as a hardened drunkard and a bold and dexterous thief. He was barefoot and bareheaded, clad in old, threadbare, shoddy breeches, in a dirty print shirt, with a torn collar that displayed his mobile, dry, angular bones tightly covered with brown skin. From the ruffled state of his black, slightly grizzled hair and the dazed look on his keen, predatory face, it was evident that he had only just waked up. There was a straw sticking in one brown mustache, another straw clung to the scrubby bristles of his shaved left cheek, and behind his ear he had stuck a little, freshly-picked twig of lime. Long, bony, rather stooping, he paced slowly over the flags, and turning his hooked, rapacious-looking nose from side to side, he cast sharp glances about him, his cold, gray eyes shining, as he scanned one after another among the dock laborers. His thick and long brown mustaches were continually twitching like a cat's whiskers, while he rubbed his hands behind his back, nervously clenching the long, crooked, clutching fingers. Even here, among hundreds of striking-looking, tattered vagabonds like himself, he attracted attention at once from his resemblance to a vulture of the steppes, from his hungry-looking thinness, and from that peculiar gait of his, as though pouncing down on his prey, so smooth and easy in appearance, but inwardly intent and alert, like the flight of the keen, nervous bird he resembled.

As he reached one of the groups of ragged dockers, reclining in the shade of a stack of coal baskets, there rose to meet him a thick-set young man, with purple blotches on his dull face and scratches on his neck, unmistakeable traces of a recent thrashing. He got up and walked beside Chelkash, saying, in an undertone:

"The dock officers have got wind of the two cases of goods. They're on the look-out. D'ye hear, Grishka?"

"What then?" queried Chelkash, cooly measuring him with his eyes.

"How 'what then?' They're on the look-out, I say. That's all."

"Did they ask for me to help them look?"

And with an acrid smile Chelkash looked toward the storehouse of the Volunteer Fleet.

"You go to the devil!"

His companion turned away.

"Ha, wait a bit! Who's been decorating you like that? Why, what a sight they have made of your signboard! Have you seen Mishka here?"

"I've not seen him this long while!" the other shouted, and hastily went back to his companions.

Chelkash went on farther, greeted by everyone as a familiar figure. But he, usually so lively and sarcastic, was unmistakeably out of humor to-day, and made short and abrupt replies to all inquiries.

From behind a pile of goods emerged a customs-house officer, a dark green, dusty figure, of military erectness. He barred the way for Chelkash, standing before him in a challenging attitude, his left hand clutching the hilt of his dirk, while with his right he tried to seize Chelkash by the collar.

"Stop! Where are you going?"

Chelkash drew back a step, raised his eyes, looked at the official, and smiled dryly.

The red, good-humoredly crafty face of the official, in its attempt to assume a menacing air, puffed and grew round and purple, while the brows scowled, the eyes rolled, and the effect was very comic.

"You've been told—don't you dare come into the dock, or I'll break your ribs! And you're here again!" the man roared threateningly.

"How d'ye do, Semyonitch! It's a long while since we've seen each other," Chelkash greeted him calmly, holding out his hand.

"Thankful never to see you again! Get along, get along!"

But yet Semyonitch took the outstretched hand.

"You tell me this," Chelkash went on, his gripping fingers still keeping their hold of Semyonitch's hand, and shaking it with friendly familiarity, "haven't you seen Mishka?"

"Mishka, indeed, who's Mishka? I don't know any Mishka. Get along, mate! or the inspector'll see you, he'll——"

"The red-haired fellow that I worked with last time on the 'Kostroma'?" Chelkash persisted.

"That you steal with, you'd better say. He's been taken to the hospital, your Mishka; his foot was crushed

by an iron bar. Go away, mate, while you're asked to
civilly, go away, or I'll chuck you out by the scruff of
your neck."

"A-ha, that's like you! And you say—you don't know
Mishka! But I say, why are you so cross, Semyonitch?"

"I tell you, Grishka, don't give me any of your jaw.
Go—o!"

The official began to get angry and, looking from side
to side, tried to pull his hand away from Chelkash's
firm grip. Chelkash looked calmly at him from under
his thick eyebrows, smiled behind his mustache, and
not letting go of his hand, went on talking.

"Don't hurry me. I'll just have my chat out with
you, and then I'll go. Come, tell us how you're getting
on; wife and children quite well?" And with a spite-
ful gleam in his eyes, he added, showing his teeth in
a mocking grin: "I've been meaning to pay you a call
for ever so long, but I've not had the time, I'm always
drinking, you see."

"Now—now then—you drop that! You—none of
your jokes, you bony devil. I'm in earnest, my man.
So you mean you're coming stealing in the houses and
the streets?"

"What for? Why there's goods enough here to last
our time—for you and me. By God, there's enough,
Semyonitch! So you've been filching two cases of
goods, eh? Mind, Semyonitch, you'd better look out!
You'll get caught one day!"

Enraged by Chelkash's insolence, Semyonitch turned
blue, and struggled, spluttering and trying to say
something. Chelkash let go of his hand, and with com-

plete composure strode back to the dock gates. The
customs-house officer followed him, swearing furiously.
Chelkash grew more cheerful; he whistled shrilly
through his teeth, and thrusting his hands in his
breeches pockets, walked with the deliberate gait of a
man of leisure, firing off to right and to left biting jeers
and jests. He was followed by retorts in the same vein.

"I say, Grishka, what good care they do take of you!
Made your inspection, eh?" shouted one out of a group
of dockers, who had finished dinner and were lying on
the ground, resting.

"I'm barefoot, so here's Semyonitch watching that I
shouldn't graze my foot on anything," answered Chelkash.

They reached the gates. Two soldiers felt Chelkash
all over, and gave him a slight shove into the streets.

"Don't let him go!" wailed Semyonitch, who had
stayed behind in the dockyard.

Chelkash crossed the road and sat down on a stone
post opposite the door of the inn. From the dock gates
rolled rumbling an endless string of laden carts. To
meet them, rattled empty carts, with their drivers jolt-
ing up and down in them. The dock vomited howling
din and biting dust, and set the earth quaking.

Chelkash, accustomed to this frenzied uproar, and
roused by his scene with Semyonitch, felt in excellent
spirits. Before him lay the attractive prospect of a sub-
stantial haul, which would call for some little exertion
and a great deal of dexterity; Chelkash was confident
that he had plenty of the latter, and, half-closing his
eyes, dreamed of how he would indulge to-morrow

morning when the business would be over and the notes would be rustling in his pocket. Then he thought of his comrade, Mishka, who would have been very useful that night, if he had not hurt his foot; Chelkash swore to himself, thinking that, all alone, without Mishka, maybe he'd hardly manage it all. What sort of night would it be? Chelkash looked at the sky, and along the street.

Half-a-dozen paces from him, on the flagged pavement, there sat, leaning against a stone post, a young fellow in a coarse blue linen shirt, and breeches of the same, in plaited bark shoes, and a torn, reddish cap. Near him lay a little bag, and a scythe without a handle, with a wisp of hay twisted round it and carefully tied with string. The youth was broad-shouldered, squarely built, flaxen headed, with a sunburnt and weather-beaten face, and big blue eyes that stared with confident simplicity at Chelkash.

Chelkash grinned at him, put out his tongue, and making a fearful face, stared persistently at him with wide-open eyes.

The young fellow at first blinked in bewilderment, but then, suddenly bursting into a guffaw, shouted through his laughter: "Oh! you funny chap!" and half getting up from the ground, rolled clumsily from his post to Chelkash's, upsetting his bag into the dust, and knocking the heel of his scythe on the stone.

"Eh, mate, you've been on the spree, one can see!" he said to Chelkash, pulling at his trousers.

"That's so, suckling, that's so indeed!" Chelkash admitted frankly; he took at once to this healthy, simple-hearted youth, with his childish clear eyes. "Been off mowing, eh?"

"To be sure! You've to mow a verst to earn ten kopecks! It's a poor business! Folks—in masses! Men had come tramping from the famine parts. They've knocked down the prices, go where you will. Sixty kopecks they paid in Kuban. And in years gone by, they do say, it was three, and four, and five roubles."

"In years gone by! Why, in years gone by, for the mere sight of a Russian they paid three roubles out that way. Ten years ago I used to make a regular trade of it. One would go to a settlement—'I'm a Russian,' one said—and they'd come and gaze at you at once, touch you, wonder at you, and—you'd get three roubles. And they'd give you food and drink—stay as long as you like!"

As the youth listened to Chelkash, at first his mouth dropped open, his round face expressing bewildered rapture; then, grasping the fact that this tattered fellow was romancing, he closed his lips with a smack and guffawed. Chelkash kept a serious face, hiding a smile in his mustache.

"You funny chap, you chaff away as though it were the truth, and I listen as if it were a bit of news! No, upon my soul, in years gone by——"

"Why, and didn't I say so? To be sure, I'm telling you how in years gone by——"

"Go on!" the lad waved his hand. "A cobbler, eh? or a tailor? or what are you?"

"I?" Chelkash queried, and after a moment's thought he said: "I'm a fisherman."

"A fi-isherman! Really? You catch fish?"

"Why fish? Fishermen about here don't catch fish only. They fish more for drowned men, old anchors, sunk ships—everything! There are hooks on purpose for all that."

"Go on! That sort of fishermen, maybe, that sing of themselves:

"We cast our nets
  Over banks that are dry,
  Over storerooms and pantries!"

"Why, have you seen any of that sort?" inquired Chelkash, looking scoffingly at him and thinking that this nice youth was very stupid.

"No, seen them I haven't! I've heard tell."

"Do you like them?"

"Like them? May be. They're all right, fine bold chaps—free."

"And what's—freedom to you? Do you care for freedom?"

"Well, I should think so! Be your own master, go where you please, do as you like. To be sure! If you know how to behave yourself, and you've nothing weighing upon you—it's first rate. Enjoy yourself all you can, only be mindful of God."

Chelkash spat contemptuously, and turning away from the youth, dropped the conversation.

"Here's my case now," the latter began, with sudden animation. "As my father's dead, my bit of land's small, my mother's old, all the land's sucked dry, what am I to do? I must live. And how? There's no telling.

"Am I to marry into some well-to-do house? I'd be glad to, if only they'd let their daughter have her share apart.

"Not a bit of it, the devil of a father-in-law won't consent to that. And so I shall have to slave for him— for ever so long—for years. A nice state of things, you know!

"But if I could earn a hundred or a hundred and fifty roubles, I could stand on my own feet, and look askance at old Antip, and tell him straight out! Will you give Marfa her share apart? No? all right, then! Thank God, she's not the only girl in the village. And I should be, I mean, quite free and independent.

"Ah, yes!" the young man sighed. "But as 'tis, there's nothing for it, but to marry and live at my father-in-law's. I was thinking I'd go, d'ye see, to Kuban, and make some two hundred roubles—straight off! Be a gentleman! But there, it was no go! It didn't come off. Well, I suppose I'll have to work for my father-in-law! Be a day-laborer. For I'll never manage on my own bit—not anyhow. Heigh-ho!"

The lad extremely disliked the idea of bondage to his future father-in-law. His face positively darkened and looked gloomy. He shifted clumsily on the ground and drew Chelkash out of the reverie into which he had sunk during his speech.

Chelkash felt that he had no inclination now to talk to him, yet he asked him another question: "Where are you going now?"

"Why, where should I go? Home, to be sure."

"Well, mate, I couldn't be sure of that, you might be on your way to Turkey."

"To Tu-urkey!" drawled the youth. "Why, what good Christian ever goes there! Well I never!"

"Oh, you fool!" sighed Chelkash, and again he turned away from his companion, conscious this time of a positive disinclination to waste another word on him. This stalwart village lad roused some feeling in him. It was a vague feeling of annoyance, that grew instinctively, stirred deep down in his heart, and hindered him from concentrating himself on the consideration of all that he had to do that night.

The lad he had thus reviled muttered something, casting occasionally a dubious glance at Chelkash. His cheeks were comically puffed out, his lips parted, and his eyes were screwed up and blinking with extreme rapidity. He had obviously not expected so rapid and insulting a termination to his conversation with this long-whiskered ragamuffin. The ragamuffin took no further notice of him. He whistled dreamily, sitting on the stone post, and beating time on it with his bare, dirty heel.

The young peasant wanted to be quits with him.

"Hi, you there, fisherman! Do you often get tipsy like this?" he was beginning, but at the same instant the fisherman turned quickly towards him, and asked:

"I say, suckling! Would you like a job to-night with me? Eh? Tell me quickly!"

"What sort of a job?" the lad asked him, distrustfully.

"What! What I set you. We're going fishing. You'll row the boat."

"Well. Yes. All right. I don't mind a job. Only there's this. I don't want to get into a mess with you. You're so awfully deep. You're rather shady."

Chelkash felt a scalding sensation in his breast, and with cold anger he said in a low voice:

"And you'd better hold your tongue, whatever you think, or I'll give you a tap on your nut that will make things light enough."

He jumped up from his post, tugged at his moustache with his left hand, while his sinewy right hand was clenched into a fist, hard as iron, and his eyes gleamed.

The youth was frightened. He looked quickly round him, and blinking uneasily, he, too, jumped up from the ground. Measuring one another with their eyes, they paused.

"Well?" Chelkash queried, sullenly. He was boiling inwardly, and trembling at the affront dealt him by this young calf, whom he had despised while he talked to him, but now hated all at once because he had such clear blue eyes, such health, a sunburned face, and broad, strong hands; because he had somewhere a village, a home in it, because a well-to-do peasant wanted him for a son-in-law, because of all his life, past and future, and most of all, because he—this babe compared with Chelkash—dared to love freedom, which he could not appreciate, nor need. It is always unpleasant to see that a man one regards as baser or lower than oneself likes or hates the same things, and so puts himself on a level with oneself.

The young peasant looked at Chelkash and saw in him an employer.

"Well," he began, "I don't mind. I'm glad of it. Why, it's work I'm looking for. I don't care whom I work for, you or any other man. I only meant that you don't look like a working man—a bit too—ragged. Oh, I know that may happen to anyone. Good Lord, as though I've never seen drunkards! Lots of them! and worse than you, too."

"All right, all right! Then you agree?" Chelkash said more amicably.

"I? Ye-es! With pleasure! Name your terms."

"That's according to the job. As the job turns out. According to our catch, that's to say. Five roubles you may get. Do you see?"

But now it was a question of money, and in that the peasant wished to be precise, and demanded the same exactness from his employer. His distrust and suspicion revived.

"That's not my way of doing business, mate! A bird in the hand for me."

Chelkash threw himself into his part.

"Don't argue, wait a bit! Come into the restaurant."

And they went down the street side by side, Chelkash with the dignified air of an employer, twisting his mustaches, the youth with an expression of absolute readiness to give way to him, but yet full of distrust and uneasiness.

"And what's your name?" asked Chelkash.

"Gavrilo!" answered the youth.

When they had come into the dirty and smoky eating-house, and Chelkash going up to the counter, in the familiar tone of an habitual customer, ordered a bottle of vodka, cabbage soup, a cut from the joint, and tea, and reckoning up his order, flung the waiter a brief "put it all down!" to which the waiter nodded in silence,—Gavrilo was at once filled with respect for this ragamuffin, his employer, who enjoyed here such an established and confident position.

"Well, now we'll have a bit of lunch and talk things over. You sit still, I'll be back in a minute."

He went out. Gavrilo looked round. The restaurant was in an underground basement; it was damp and dark, and reeked with the stifling fumes of vodka, to-bacco-smoke, tar, and some acrid odor. Facing Gavrilo at another table sat a drunken man in the dress of a sailor, with a red beard, all over coal-dust and tar. Hiccupping every minute, he was droning a song all made up of broken and incoherent words, strangely sibilant and guttural sounds. He was unmistakably not a Russian.

Behind him sat two Moldavian women, tattered, black-haired sunburned creatures, who were chanting some sort of song, too, with drunken voices.

And from the darkness beyond emerged other figures, all strangely dishevelled, all half-drunk, noisy and rest-less.

Gavrilo felt miserable here alone. He longed for his employer to come back quickly. And the din in the eating-house got louder and louder. Growing shriller every second, it all melted into one note, and it seemed like the roaring of some monstrous beast, with hundreds of different throats, vaguely enraged, trying to struggle out of this damp hole and unable to find a way out to freedom. Gavrilo felt something intoxicating and oppressive creeping over him, over all his limbs, making his head reel, and his eyes grow dim, as they moved inquisitively about the eating-house.

Chelkash came in, and they began eating and drinking and talking. At the third glass Gavrilo was drunk. He became lively and wanted to say something pleasant to his employer, who—the good fellow!—though he had done nothing for him yet, was entertaining him so agreeably. But the words which flowed in perfect waves to his throat, for some reason would not come from his tongue.

Chelkash looked at him and smiled sarcastically, saying:

"You're screwed! Ugh—milksop!—with five glasses! how will you work?"

"Dear fellow!" Gavrilo melted into a drunken, good-natured smile. "Never fear! I respect you! That is, look here! Let me kiss you! eh?"

"Come, come! A drop more!"

Gavrilo drank, and at last reached a condition when everything seemed waving up and down in regular undulations before his eyes. It was unpleasant and made him feel sick. His face wore an expression of childish bewilderment and foolish enthusiasm. Trying to say something, he smacked his lips absurdly and bellowed. Chelkash, watching him intently, twisted his mustaches, and as though recollecting something, still smiled to himself, but morosely now and maliciously.

The eating-house roared with drunken clamor. The red-headed sailor was asleep, with his elbows on the table.

"Come, let's go then!" said Chelkash, getting up.

Gavrilo tried to get up, but could not, and with a vigorous oath, he laughed a meaningless, drunken laugh.

"Quite screwed!" said Chelkash, sitting down again opposite him.

Gavrilo still guffawed, staring with dull eyes at his new employer. And the latter gazed at him intently, vigilantly and thoughtfully. He saw before him a man whose life had fallen into his wolfish clutches. He, Chelkash, felt that he had the power to do with it as he pleased. He could rend it like a card, and he could help to set it on a firm footing in its peasant framework. He revelled in feeling himself master of another man, and thought that never would this peasant-lad drink of such a cup as destiny had given him, Chelkash, to drink. And he envied this young life and pitied it, sneered at it, and was even troubled over it, picturing to himself how it might again fall into such hands as his.

And all these feelings in the end melted in Chelkash into one—a fatherly sense of proprietorship in him. He felt sorry for the boy, and the boy was necessary to him. Then Chelkash took Gavrilo under the arms, and giving him a slight shove behind with his knee, got him out into the yard of the eating-house, where he put him on the ground in the shade of a stack of wood, then he sat down beside him and lighted his pipe.

Gavrilo shifted about a little, muttered, and dropped asleep.

CHAPTER II.

"COME, ready?" Chelkash asked in a low voice of Gavrilo, who was busy doing something to the oars.

"In a minute! The rowlock here's unsteady, can I just knock it in with the oar?"

"No—no! Not a sound! Push it down harder with your hand, it'll go in of itself."

They were both quietly getting out a boat, which was tied to the stern of one of a whole flotilla of oak-laden barges, and big Turkish feluccas, half unloaded, half still full of palm-oil, sandal wood, and thick trunks of cypress.

The night was dark, thick strata of ragged clouds were moving across the sky, and the sea was quiet, black, and thick as oil. It wafted a damp and salt aroma, and splashed caressingly on the sides of the vessels and the banks, setting Chelkash's boat lightly rocking. There were boats all round them. At a long distance from the shore rose from the sea the dark outlines of vessels, thrusting up into the dark sky their pointed masts with various colored lights at their tops. The sea reflected the lights, and was spotted with masses of yellow, quivering patches. This was very beautiful on the velvety bosom of the soft, dull black water, so rhythmically, mightily breathing. The sea slept the sound, healthy sleep of a workman, wearied out by his day's toil.

"We're off!" said Gavrilo, dropping the oars into the water.

"Yes!" With a vigorous turn of the rudder Chelkash drove the boat into a strip of water between two barks, and they darted rapidly over the smooth surface, that kindled into bluish phosphorescent light under the strokes of the oars. Behind the boat's stern lay a winding ribbon of this phosphorescence, broad and quivering.

"Well, how's your head, aching?" asked Chelkash, smiling.

"Awfully! Like iron ringing. I'll wet it with some water in a minute."

"Why? You'd better wet your inside, that may get rid of it. You can do that at once." He held out a bottle to Gavrilo.

"Eh? Lord bless you!"

There was a faint sound of swallowing.

"Aye! aye! like it? Enough!" Chelkash stopped him.

The boat darted on again, noiselessly and lightly threading its way among the vessels. All at once, they emerged from the labyrinth of ships, and the sea, boundless, mute, shining and rhythmically breathing, lay open before them, stretching far into the distance, where there rose out of its waters masses of storm clouds, some lilac-blue with fluffy yellow edges, and some greenish like the color of the seawater, or those dismal, leaden-colored clouds that cast such heavy, dreary shadows, oppressing mind and soul. They crawled slowly after one another, one melting into another, one overtaking another, and there was something weird in this slow procession of soulless masses. It seemed as though there, at the sea's rim, they were a countless multitude, that they would forever crawl thus sluggishly over the sky, striving with dull malignance to hinder it from peeping at the sleeping sea with its millions of golden eyes, the various colored, vivid stars, that shine so dreamily and stir high hopes in all who love their pure, holy light. Over the sea hovered the vague, soft sound of its drowsy breathing.

"The sea's fine, eh?" asked Chelkash.

"It's all right! Only I feel scared on it," answered Gavrilo, pressing the oars vigorously and evenly through the water. The water faintly gurgled and splashed under the strokes of his long oars, splashed glittering with the warm, bluish, phosphorescent light.

"Scared! What a fool!" Chelkash muttered, discontentedly.

He, the thief and cynic, loved the sea. His effervescent, nervous nature, greedy after impressions, was never weary of gazing at that dark expanse, boundless, free, and mighty. And it hurt him to hear such an answer to his question about the beauty of what he loved. Sitting in the stern, he cleft the water with his oar, and looked on ahead quietly, filled with desire to glide far on this velvety surface, not soon to quit it.

On the sea there always rose up in him a broad, warm feeling, that took possession of his whole soul, and somewhat purified it from the sordidness of daily life. He valued this, and loved to feel himself better out here in the midst of the water and the air, where the cares of life, and life itself, always lose, the former their keenness, the latter its value.

"But where's the tackle? Eh?" Gavrilo asked suspiciously all at once, peering into the boat.

Chelkash started.

"Tackle? I've got it in the stern."

"Why, what sort of tackle is it?" Gavrilo inquired again with surprised suspicion in his tone.

"What sort? lines and—" But Chelkash felt ashamed to lie to this boy, to conceal his real plans, and he was sorry to lose what this peasant-lad had destroyed in his heart by this question. He flew into a rage. That scalding bitterness he knew so well rose in his breast and his throat, and impressively, cruelly, and malignantly he said to Gavrilo:

"You're sitting here—and I tell you, you'd better sit quiet. And not poke your nose into what's not your business. You've been hired to row, and you'd better row. But if you can't keep your tongue from wagging, it will be a bad lookout for you. D'ye see?"

For a minute the boat quivered and stopped. The oars rested in the water, setting it foaming, and Gavrilo moved uneasily on his seat.

"Row!"

A sharp oath rang out in the air. Gavrilo swung the oars. The boat moved with rapid, irregular jerks, noisily cutting the water.

"Steady!"

Chelkash got up from the stern, still holding the oars in his hands, and peering with his cold eyes into the pale and twitching face of Gavrilo. Crouching forward Chelkash was like a cat on the point of spring-ing. There was the sound of angry gnashing of teeth.

"Who's calling?" rang out a surly shout from the sea.

"Now, you devil, row! quietly with the oars! I'll kill you, you cur. Come, row! One, two! There! you only make a sound! I'll cut your throat!" hissed Chel-kash.

"Mother of God—Holy Virgin—" muttered Gavrilo, shaking and numb with terror and exertion.

The boat turned smoothly and went back toward the harbor, where the lights gathered more closely into a group of many colors and the straight stems of masts could be seen.

"Hi! Who's shouting?" floated across again. The voice was farther off this time. Chelkash grew calm again.

"It's yourself, friend, that's shouting!" he said in the direction of the shouts, and then he turned to Gav-rilo, who was muttering a prayer.

"Well, mate, you're in luck! If those devils had over-taken us, it would have been all over with you. D'you see? I'd have you over in a trice—to the fishes!"

Now, when Chelkash was speaking quietly and even good-humoredly, Gavrilo, still shaking with terror, be-sought him!

"Listen, forgive me! For Christ's sake, I beg you, let me go! Put me on shore somewhere! Aïe-aïe-aïe! I'm done for entirely! Come, think of God, let me go! What am I to you? I can't do it! I've never been used to such things. It's the first time. Lord! Why, I shall be lost! How did you get round me, mate? eh?

It's a shame of you! Why, you're ruining a man's life! Such doings."

"What doings?" Chelkash asked grimly. "Eh? Well, what doings?"

He was amused by the youth's terror, and he enjoyed it and the sense that he, Chelkash, was a terrible person.

"Shady doings, mate. Let me go, for God's sake! What am I to you? eh? Good—dear—!"

"Hold your tongue, do! If you weren't wanted, I shouldn't have taken you. Do you understand? So, shut up!"

"Lord!" Gavrilo sighed, sobbing.

"Come, come! you'd better mind!" Chelkash cut him short.

But Gavrilo by now could not restrain himself, and quietly sobbing, he wept, sniffed, and writhed in his seat, yet rowed vigorously, desperately. The boat shot on like an arrow. Again dark hulks of ships rose up on their way and the boat was again lost among them, winding like a wolf in the narrow lanes of water between them.

"Here, you listen! If anyone asks you anything,— hold your tongue, if you want to get off alive! Do you see?"

"Oh—oh!" Gavrilo sighed hopelessly in answer to the grim advice, and bitterly he added: "I'm a lost man!"

"Don't howl!" Chelkash whispered impressively.

This whisper deprived Gavrilo of all power of grasping anything and transformed him into a senseless automaton, wholly absorbed in a chill presentiment of calamity. Mechanically he lowered the oars into the water, threw himself back, drew them out and dropped them in again, all the while staring blankly at his plaited shoes. The waves splashed against the vessels with a sort of menace, a sort of warning in their drowsy sound that terrified him. The dock was reached. From its granite wall came the sound of men's voices, the splash of water, singing, and shrill whistles.

"Stop!" whispered Chelkash. "Give over rowing! Push along with your hands on the wall! Quietly, you devil!"

Gavrilo, clutching at the slippery stone, pushed the boat alongside the wall. The boat moved without a sound, sliding alongside the green, shiny stone.

"Stop! Give me the oars! Give them here. Where's your passport? In the bag? Give me the bag! Come, give it here quickly! That, my dear fellow, is so you shouldn't run off. You won't run away now. Without oars you might have got off somehow, but without a passport you'll be afraid to. Wait here! But mind— if you squeak—to the bottom of the sea you go!"

And, all at once, clinging on to something with his hands, Chelkash rose in the air and vanished onto the wall.

Gavrilo shuddered. It had all happened so quickly. He felt as though the cursed weight and horror that had crushed him in the presence of this thin thief with his mustaches was loosened and rolling off him. Now to run! And breathing freely, he looked round him. On his left rose a black hulk, without masts, a sort of huge coffin, mute, untenanted, and desolate. Every splash of the water on its sides awakened a hollow, resonant echo within it, like a heavy sigh.

On the right the damp stone wall of the quay trailed its length, winding like a heavy, chill serpent. Behind him, too, could be seen black blurs of some sort, while in front, in the opening between the wall and the side of that coffin, he could see the sea, a silent waste, with the storm-clouds crawling above it. Everything was cold, black, malignant. Gavrilo felt panic-stricken. This terror was worse than the terror inspired in him by Chelkash; it penetrated into Gavrilo's bosom with icy keenness, huddled him into a cowering mass, and kept him nailed to his seat in the boat.

All around was silent. Not a sound but the sighs of the sea, and it seemed as though this silence would instantly be rent by something fearful, furiously loud, something that would shake the sea to its depths, tear apart these heavy flocks of clouds on the sky, and scatter all these black ships. The clouds were crawling over the sky as dismally as before; more of them still rose up out of the sea, and, gazing at the sky, one might believe that it, too, was a sea, but a sea in agitation, and grown petrified in its agitation, laid over that other sea beneath, that was so drowsy, serene, and smooth. The clouds were like waves, flinging themselves with curly gray crests down upon the earth and into the abysses of space, from which they were torn again by the wind, and tossed back upon the rising billows of cloud, that were not yet hidden under the greenish foam of their furious agitation.

Gavrilo felt crushed by this gloomy stillness and beauty, and felt that he longed to see his master come back quickly. And how was it that he lingered there so long? The time passed slowly, more slowly than those clouds crawled over the sky. And the stillness grew more malignant as time went on. From the wall of the quay came the sound of splashing, rustling, and something like whispering. It seemed to Gavrilo that he would die that moment.

"Hi! Asleep? Hold it! Carefully!" sounded the hollow voice of Chelkash.

From the wall something cubical and heavy was let down. Gavrilo took it into the boat. Something else like it followed. Then across the wall stretched Chelkash's long figure, the oars appeared from somewhere, Gavrilo's bag dropped at his feet, and Chelkash, breathing heavily, settled himself in the stern.

Gavrilo gazed at him with a glad and timid smile.

"Tired?"

"Bound to be that, calf! Come now, row your best! Put your back into it! You've earned good wages, mate. Half the job's done. Now we've only to slip under the devils' noses, and then you can take your money and go off to your Mashka. You've got a Mashka, I suppose, eh, kiddy?"

"N—no!" Gavrilo strained himself to the utmost, working his chest like a pair of bellows, and his arms like steel springs. The water gurgled under the boat, and the blue streak behind the stern was broader now. Gavrilo was soaked through with sweat at once, but he still rowed on with all his might. After living through such terror twice that night, he dreaded now having to go through it a third time, and longed for one thing only—to make an end quickly of this accursed task, to get on to land, and to run away from this man, before he really did kill him, or get him into prison. He resolved not to speak to him about anything, not to contradict him, to do all he told him, and, if he should succeed in getting successfully quit of him, to pay for a thanksgiving service to be said to-morrow to Nikolai the Wonder-worker. A passionate prayer was ready to burst out from his bosom. But he restrained himself, puffed like a steamer, and was silent, glancing from under his brows at Chelkash.

The latter, with his lean, long figure bent forward like a bird about to take flight, stared into the darkness ahead of the boat with his hawk eyes, and turning his rapacious, hooked nose from side to side, gripped with one hand the rudder handle, while with the other he twirled his mustache, that was continually quivering with smiles. Chelkash was pleased with his success, with himself, and with this youth, who had been so frightened of him and had been turned into his slave. He had a vision of unstinted dissipation to-morrow, while now he enjoyed the sense of his strength, which had enslaved this young, fresh lad. He watched how he was toiling, and felt sorry for him, wanted to encourage him.

"Eh!" he said softly, with a grin. "Were you awfully scared? eh?"

"Oh, no!" sighed Gavrilo, and he cleared his throat.

"But now you needn't work so at the oars. Ease

off! There's only one place now to pass. Rest a bit."

Gavrilo obediently paused, rubbed the sweat off his face with the sleeve of his shirt, and dropped the oars again into the water.

"Now, row more slowly, so that the water shouldn't bubble. We've only the gates to pass. Softly, softly. For they're serious people here, mate. They might take a pop at one in a minute. They'd give you such a bump on your forehead, you wouldn't have time to call out."

The boat now crept along over the water almost without a sound. Only from the oars dripped blue drops of water, and when they trickled into the sea, a blue patch of light was kindled for a minute where they fell. The night had become still warmer and more silent. The sky was no longer like a sea in turmoil, the clouds were spread out and covered it with a smooth, heavy canopy that hung low over the water and did not stir. And the sea was still more calm and black, and stronger than ever was the warm salt smell from it.

"Ah, if only it would rain!" whispered Chelkash. "We could get through then, behind a curtain as it were."

On the right and the left of the boat, like houses rising out of the black water, stood barges, black, motionless, and gloomy. On one of them moved a light; some one was walking up and down with a lantern. The sea stroked their sides with a hollow sound of supplication, and they responded with an echo, cold and resonant, as though unwilling to yield anything.

"The coastguards!" Chelkash whispered hardly above a breath.

From the moment when he had bidden him row more slowly, Gavrilo had again been overcome by that intense agony of expectation. He craned forward into the darkness, and he felt as though he were growing bigger; his bones and sinews were strained with a dull ache, his head, filled with a single idea, ached, the skin on his back twitched, and his legs seemed pricked with sharp, chill little pins and needles. His eyes ached from the strain of gazing into the darkness, whence he expected every instant something would spring up and shout to them: "Stop, thieves!"

Now when Chelkash whispered: "The coastguards!" Gavrilo shuddered, and one intense, burning idea passed through him, and thrilled his overstrained nerves; he longed to cry out, to call men to his aid. He opened his mouth, and half rose from his seat, squared his chest, drew in a full draught of breath—and opened his mouth—but suddenly, struck down by a terror that smote him like a whip, he shut his eyes and rolled forward off his seat.

Far away on the horizon, ahead of the boat, there rose up out of the black water of the sea a huge fiery blue sword; it rose up, cleaving the darkness of night, its blade glided through the clouds in the sky, and lay, a broad blue streak on the bosom of the sea. It lay there, and in the streak of its light there sprang up out of the darkness ships unseen till then, black and mute, shrouded in the thick night mist. It seemed as though they had lain long at the bottom of the sea, dragged down by the mighty hands of the tempest; and now behold they had been drawn up by the power and at the will of this blue fiery sword, born of the sea— had been drawn up to gaze upon the sky and all that was above the water. Their rigging wrapped about the masts and looked like clinging seaweeds, that had risen from the depths with these black giants caught in their snares. And it rose upward again from the sea, this strange blue sword,—rose, cleft the night again, and again fell down in another direction. And again, where it lay, there rose up out of the dark the outlines of vessels, unseen before.

Chelkash's boat stopped and rocked on the water, as though in uncertainty. Gavrilo lay at the bottom, his face hidden in his hands, until Chelkash poked him with an oar and whispered furiously, but softly:

"Fool, it's the customs cruiser. That's the electric light! Get up, blockhead! Why, they'll turn the light on us in a minute! You'll be the ruin of yourself and me! Come!"

And at last, when a blow from the sharp end of the oar struck Gavrilo's head more violently, he jumped up, still afraid to open his eyes, sat down on the seat, and, fumbling for the oars, rowed the boat on.

"Quietly! I'll kill you! Didn't I tell you? There, quietly! Ah, you fool, damn you! What are you frightened of? Eh, pig face? A lantern and a reflector, that's all it is. Softly with the oars! Mawkish devil! They turn the reflector this way and that way, and light up the sea, so as to see if there are folks like you and me afloat. To catch smugglers, they do it. They won't get us, they've sailed too far off. Don't be frightened, lad, they won't catch us. Now we——" Chelkash looked triumphantly round. "It's over, we've rowed out of reach! Foo—o! Come, you're in luck."

Gavrilo sat mute; he rowed, and breathing hard, looked askance where that fiery sword still rose and sank. He was utterly unable to believe Chelkash that it was only a lantern and a reflector. The cold, blue brilliance, that cut through the darkness and made the sea gleam with silver light, had something about it inexplicable, portentous, and Gavrilo now sank into a sort of hypnotized, miserable terror. Some vague presentiment weighed aching on his breast. He rowed automatically, with pale face, huddled up as though expecting a blow from above, and there was no thought, no desire in him now, he was empty and soulless. The emotions of that night had swallowed up at last all that was human in him.

But Chelkash was triumphant again; complete success! all anxiety at an end! His nerves, accustomed to strain, relaxed, returned to the normal. His mustaches twitched voluptuously, and there was an eager light in his eyes. He felt splendid, whistled through his teeth, drew in deep breaths of the damp sea air, looked about him in the darkness, and laughed good-naturedly when his eyes rested on Gavrilo.

The wind blew up and waked the sea into a sudden play of fine ripples. The clouds had become, as it were, finer and more transparent, but the sky was still covered with them. The wind, though still light, blew freely over the sea, yet the clouds were motionless and seemed plunged in some gray, dreary dream.

"Come, mate, pull yourself together! it's high time! Why, what a fellow you are; as though all the breath had been knocked out of your skin, and only a bag of bones was left! My dear fellow! It's all over now! Hey!"

It was pleasant to Gavrilo to hear a human voice, even though Chelkash it was that spoke.

"I hear," he said softly.

"Come, then, milksop. Come, you sit at the rudder and I'll take the oars, you must be tired!"

Mechanically Gavrilo changed places. When Chelkash, as he changed places with him, glanced into his face, and noticed that he was staggering on his shaking legs, he felt still sorrier for the lad. He clapped him on the shoulder.

"Come, come, don't be scared! You've earned a good sum for it. I'll pay you richly, mate. Would you like twenty-five roubles, eh?"

"I—don't want anything. Only to be on shore."

Chelkash waved his hand, spat, and fell to rowing, flinging the oars far back with his long arms.

The sea had waked up. It frolicked in little waves, bringing them forth, decking them with a fringe of foam, flinging them on one another, and breaking them up into tiny eddies. The foam, melting, hissed and sighed, and everything was filled with the musical plash and cadence. The darkness seemed more alive.

"Come, tell me," began Chelkash, "you'll go home to the village, and you'll marry and begin digging the

earth and sowing corn, your wife will bear you children, food won't be too plentiful, and so you'll grind
away all your life. Well? Is there such sweetness in
that?"

"Sweetness!" Gavrilo answered, timid and trembl-
ling, "what, indeed?"

The wind tore a rent in the clouds and through the
gap peeped blue bits of sky, with one or two stars.
Reflected in the frolicking sea, these stars danced on
the waves, vanishing and shining out again.

"More to the right!" said Chelkash. "Soon we shall
be there. Well, well! It's over. A haul that's worth
it! See here. One night, and I've made five hundred
roubles! Eh? What do you say to that?"

"Five hundred?" Gavrilo, drawled, incredulously, but
he was scared at once, and quickly asked, prodding the
bundle in the boat with his foot. "Why, what sort
of thing may this be?"

"That's silk. A costly thing. All that, if one sold
it for its value, would fetch a thousand. But I sell
cheap. Is that smart business?"

"I sa—ay?" Gavrilo drawled dubiously. "If only I'd
all that!" he sighed, recalling all at once the village, his
poor little bit of land, his poverty, his mother, and all
that was so far away and so near his heart; for the
sake of which he had gone to seek work, for the sake
of which he had suffered such agonies that night. A
flood of memories came back to him of his village, running down the steep slope to the river and losing itself
in a whole forest of birch trees, willows, and mountain-
ashes. These memories breathed something warm into

him and cheered him up. "Ah, it would be grand!" he sighed mournfully.

"To be sure! I expect you'd bolt home by the railway! And wouldn't the girls make love to you at home, aye, aye! You could choose which you liked! You'd build yourself a house. No, the money, maybe, would hardly be enough for a house."

"That's true—it wouldn't do for a house. Wood's dear down our way."

"Well, never mind. You'd mend up the old one. How about a horse? Have you got one?"

"A horse? Yes, I have, but a wretched old thing it is."

"Well, then, you'd have a horse. A first-rate horse! A cow—sheep—fowls of all sorts. Eh?"

"Don't talk of it! If I only could! Oh, Lord! What a life I should have!"

"Aye, mate, your life would be first-rate. I know something about such things. I had a home of my own once. My father was one of the richest in the village."

Chelkash rowed slowly. The boat danced on the waves that sportively splashed over its edge; it scarcely moved forward on the dark sea; which frolicked more and more gayly. The two men were dreaming, rocked on the water, and pensively looking around them. Chelkash had turned Gavrilo's thoughts to his village with the aim of encouraging and reassuring him. At first he had talked grinning sceptically to himself under his mustaches, but afterward, as he replied to his companion and reminded him of the joys of a peasant's life, which he had so long ago wearied of, had forgotten, and only now recalled, he was gradually carried away, and, instead of questioning the peasant youth about his village and its doings, unconsciously he dropped into describing it himself:

"The great thing in the peasant's life, mate, is its freedom! You're your own master. You've your own home—worth a farthing, maybe—but it's yours! You've your own land—only a handful the whole of it—but it's yours! Hens of your own, eggs, apples of your own! You're king on your own land! And then the regularity. You get up in the morning, you've work to do, in the spring one sort, in the summer another, in the autumn, in the winter—different again. Wherever you go, you've home to come back to! It's snug! There's peace! You're a king! Aren't you really?" Chelkash concluded enthusiastically his long reckoning of the peasant's advantages and privileges, forgetting, somehow, his duties.

Gavrilo looked at him with curiosity, and he, too, warmed to the subject. During this conversation he had succeeded in forgetting with whom he had to deal, and he saw in his companion a peasant like himself—cemented to the soil for ever by the sweat of generations, and bound to it by the recollections of childhood—who had wilfully broken loose from it and from its cares, and was bearing the inevitable punishment for this abandonment.

"That's true, brother! Ah, how true it is! Look at you, now, what you've become away from the land! Aha! The land, brother, is like a mother, you can't forget it for long."

Chelkash awaked from his reverie. He felt that scalding irritation in his chest, which always came as soon as his pride, the pride of the reckless vagrant, was touched by anyone, and especially by one who was of no value in his eyes.

"His tongue's set wagging!" he said savagely, "you thought, maybe, I said all that in earnest. Never fear!"

"But, you strange fellow!"—Gavrilo began, overawed again—"Was I speaking of you? Why, there's lots like you! Ah, what a lot of unlucky people among the people! Wanderers——"

"Take the oars, you sea-calf!" Chelkash commanded briefly, for some reason holding back a whole torrent of furious abuse, which surged up into his throat.

They changed places again, and Chelkash, as he crept across the boat to the stern, felt an intense desire to give Gavrilo a kick that would send him flying into the water, and at the same time could not pluck up courage to look him in the face.

The brief conversation dropped, but now Gavrilo's silence even was eloquent of the country to Chelkash. He recalled the past, and forgot to steer the boat, which was turned by the current and floated away out to sea. The waves seemed to understand that this boat had missed its way, and played lightly with it, tossing it higher and higher, and kindling their gay blue light under its oars. While before Chelkash's eyes floated pictures of the past, the far past, separated from the present by the whole barrier of eleven years of vagrant life. He saw himself a child, his village, his mother, a red-cheeked plump woman, with kindly gray eyes, his father, a red-bearded giant with a stern face. He saw himself betrothed, and saw his wife, black-eyed Anfisa, with her long hair, plump, mild, and good-humored; again himself a handsome soldier in the Guards; again his father, gray now and bent with toil, and his mother wrinkled and bowed to the ground; he saw, too, the picture of his welcome in the village when he returned from the service; saw how proud his father was before all the village of his Grigory, the mustached, stalwart soldier, so smart and handsome. Memory, the scourge of the unhappy, gives life to the very stones of the past, and even into the poison drunk in old days pours drops of honey, so as to confound a man with his mistakes and, by making him love the past, rob him of hope for the future.

Chelkash felt a rush of the softening, caressing air of home, bringing back to him the tender words of his mother and the weighty utterances of the venerable peasant, his father; many a forgotten sound and many a lush smell of mother-earth, freshly thawing, freshly ploughed, and freshly covered with the emerald silk of the corn. And he felt crushed, lost, pitiful, and solitary, torn up and cast out for ever from that life which had distilled the very blood that flowed in his veins.

"Hey! but where are we going?" Gavrilo asked suddenly.

Chelkash started and looked round with the uneasy look of a bird of prey.

"Ah, the devil's taken the boat! No matter. Row a bit harder. We'll be there directly."

"You were dreaming?" Gavrilo inquired, smiling.

Chelkash looked searchingly at him. The youth had completely regained his composure; he was calm, cheerful and even seemed somehow triumphant. He was very young, all his life lay before him. And he knew nothing. That was bad. Maybe the earth would keep hold of him. As these thoughts flashed through his head, Chelkash felt still more mournful, and to Gavrilo he jerked out sullenly:

"I'm tired. And it rocks, too."

"It does rock, that's true. But now, I suppose, we shan't get caught with this?" Gavrilo shoved the bale with his foot.

"No. You can be easy. I shall hand it over directly and get the money. Oh, yes!"

"Five hundred?"

"Not less, I dare say."

"I say—that's a sum! If I, poor wretch, had that! Ah, I'd have a fine time with it."

"On your land?"

"To be sure! Why, I'd be off——"

And Gravilo floated off into day dreams. Chelkash seemed crushed. His mustaches drooped, his right side was soaked by the splashing of the waves, his eyes looked sunken and had lost their brightness. He was a pitiable and depressed figure. All that bird-of-prey look in his figure seemed somehow eclipsed under a humiliated moodiness, that showed itself in the very folds of his dirty shirt.

"I'm tired out, too—regularly done up."

"We'll be there directly. See over yonder."

Chelkash turned the boat sharply, and steered it toward something black that stood up out of the water.

The sky was again all covered with clouds, and fine, warm rain had come on, pattering gayly on the crests of the waves.

"Stop! easy!" commanded Chelkosh.

The boat's nose knocked against the hull of the vessel.

"Are they asleep, the devils?" grumbled Chelkash, catching with his boat-hook on to some ropes that hung over the ship's side. "The ladder's not down. And this rain, too. As if it couldn't have come before! Hi, you spongeos. Hi! Hi!"

"Is that Selkash?" they heard a soft purring voice say overhead.

"Come, let down the ladder."

"Kalimera, Selkash."

"Let down the ladder, you smutty devil!" yelled Chelkash.

"Ah, what a rage he's come in to-day. Ahoy!"

"Get up, Gavrilo!" Chelkash said to his companion.

In a moment they were on the deck, where three dark-bearded figures, eagerly chattering together, in a strange staccato tongue looked over the side into Chelkash's boat. The fourth clad in a long gown, went up to him and pressed his hand without speaking, then looked suspiciously round at Gavrilo.

"Get the money ready for me by the morning," Chelkash said to him shortly. "And now I'll go to sleep. Gavrilo, come along! Are you hungry?"

"I'm sleepy," answered Gavrilo, and five minutes later he was snoring in the dirty hold of the vessel, while

Chelkash, sitting beside him, tried on somebody's boots. Dreamily spitting on one side, he whistled angrily and mournfully between his teeth. Then he stretched himself out beside Gavrilo, and pulling the boots off his feet again and putting his arms under his head, he fell to gazing intently at the deck, and pulling his mustaches.

The vessel rocked softly on the frolicking water, there was a fretful creaking of wood somewhere, the rain pattered softly on the deck, and the waves splashed on the ship's side. Everything was melancholy and sounded like the lullaby of a mother. who has no hope of her child's happiness. And Chelkash fell asleep.

CHAPTER III

HE was the first to wake, he looked round him uneasily, but at once regained his self-possession and stared at Gavrilo who was still asleep. He was sweetly snoring, and in his sleep smiled all over his childish, sunburned healthy face. Chelkash sighed and climbed up the narrow rope-ladder. Through the port-hole he saw a leaden strip of sky. It was daylight, but a dreary autumn grayness.

Chelkash came back, two hours later. His face was red, his mustaches were jauntily curled, a smile of good-humored gayety beamed on his lips. He was wearing a pair of stout high boots, a short jacket, and leather breeches, and he looked like a sportsman. His whole costume was worn, but strong, and very becoming to him, making him look broader, covering up his angularity, and giving him a military air.

"Hi, little calf, get up!" He gave Gavrilo a kick.

Gavrilo started up, and, not recognizing him, stared at him in alarm with dull eyes. Chelkash chuckled.

"Well, you do look——" Gavrilo brought out with a broad grin at last. "You're quite a gentleman!"

"We soon change. But, I say, you're easily scared! aye! How many times were you ready to die last night? eh? tell me!"

"Well, but just think, it's the first time I've ever been on such a job! Why one may lose one's soul for all one's life!"

"Well, would you go again? Eh?"

"Again? Well—that—how can I say? For what inducement? That's the point!"

"Well, if it were for two rainbows?"

"Two hundred roubles, you mean? Well—I might."

"But I say! What about your soul?"

"Oh, well—maybe one wouldn't lose it!" Gavrilo smiled. "One mightn't—and it would make a man of one for all one's life."

Chelkash laughed good-humoredly.

"All right! that's enough joking. Let's row to land. Get ready!"

"Why, I've nothing to do! I'm ready."

And soon they were in the boat again, Chelkash at the rudder, Gavrilo at the oars. Above them the sky was gray, with clouds stretched evenly across it. The muddy green sea played with their boat, tossing it noisily on the waves that sportively flung bright salt drops into it. Far ahead from the boat's prow could be seen the yellow streak of the sandy shore, while from the stern there stretched away into the distance the free, gambolling sea, all furrowed over with racing flocks of billows, decked here and there with a narrow fringe of foam. Far away they could see numbers of vessels, rocking on the bosom of the sea, away on the left a whole forest of masts and the white fronts of the houses of the town. From that direction there floated across the sea a dull resounding roar, that mingled with the splash of the waves into a full rich music. And over all was flung a delicate veil of ash-colored mist, that made things seem far from one another.

"Ah, there'll be a pretty dance by evening!" said Chelkash, nodding his head at the sea.

"A storm?" queried Gavrilo, working vigorously at the waves with his oars. He was already wet through from head to foot with the splashing the wind blew on him from the sea.

"Aye, aye!" Chelkash assented.

Gavrilo looked inquisitively at him, and his eyes expressed unmistakeable expectation of something.

"Well, how much did they give you?" he asked, at last, seeing that Chelkash was not going to begin the conversation.

"Look!" said Chelkash, holding out to Gavrilo something he had pulled out of his pocket.

Gavrilo saw the rainbow-colored notes and everything danced in brilliant rainbow tints before his eyes.

"I say! Why, I thought you were bragging! That's —how much?"

"Five hundred and forty! A smart job!"

"Smart, yes!" muttered Gavrilo, with greedy eyes,

watching the five hundred and forty roubles as they were put back again in his pocket. "Well, I never! What a lot of money!" and he sighed dejectedly.

"We'll have a jolly good spree, my lad!" Chelkash cried ecstatically. "Eh, we've enough to. Never fear, mate, I'll give you your share. I'll give you forty, eh? Satisfied? If you like, I'll give it you now!"

"If—you don't mind. Well? I wouldn't say no!"

Gavrilo was trembling all over with suspense and some other acute feeling that dragged at his heart.

"Ha—ha—ha! Oh, you devil's doll! 'I'd not say no!' Take it, mate, please! I beg you, indeed, take it! I don't know what to do with such a lot of money! You must help me out, take some, there!"

Chelkash held out some red notes to Gavrilo. He took them with a shaking hand, let go the oars, and began stuffing them away in his bosom, greedily screwing up his eyes and drawing in his breath noisily, as though he had drunk something hot. Chelkash watched him with an ironical smile. Gavrilo took up the oars again and rowed nervously, hurriedly, keeping his eyes down as though he were afraid of something. His shoulders and his ears were twitching.

"You're greedy. That's bad. But, of course, you're a peasant," Chelkash said musingly.

"But see what one can do with money!" cried Gavrilo, suddenly breaking into passionate excitement, and jerkily, hurriedly, as though chasing his thoughts and catching his words as they flew, he began to speak of life in the village with money and without money. Respect, plenty, independence gladness!

Chelkash heard him attentively, with a serious face and eyes filled with some dreamy thought. At times he smiled a smile of content. "Here we are!" Chelkash cried at last, interrupting Gavrilo.

A wave caught up the boat and neatly drove it onto the sand.

"Come, mate, now it's over. We must drag the boat up farther, so that it shouldn't get washed away. They'll come and fetch it. Well, we must say good-bye! It's eight versts from here to the town. What are you going to do? Coming back to the town, eh?"

Chelkash's face was radiant with a good-humoredly sly smile, and altogether he had the air of a man who had thought of something very pleasant for himself and a surprise to Gavrilo. Thrusting his hand into his pocket, he rustled the notes there.

"No—I—am not coming. I——" Gavrilo gasped, and seemed choking with something. Within him there was raging a whole storm of desires, of words, of feelings, that swallowed up one another and scorched him as with fire.

Chelkash looked at him in perplexity.

"What's the matter with you?" he asked.

"Why——" But Gavrilo's face flushed, then turned gray, and he moved irresolutely, as though he were half longing to throw himself on Chelkash, or half torn by some desire, the attainment of which was hard for him.

Chelkash felt ill at ease at the sight of such excitement in this lad. He wondered what form it would take.

Gavrilo began laughing strangely, a laugh that was

like a sob. His head was downcast, the expression of his face Chelkash could not see; Gavrilo's ears only were dimly visible, and they turned red and then pale.

"Well, damn you!" Chelkash waved his hand, "Have you fallen in love with me, or what? One might think you were a girl! Or is parting from me so upsetting? Hey, suckling! Tell me, what's wrong? or else I'm off!"

"You're going!" Gavrilo cried aloud.

The sandy waste of the shore seemed to start at his cry, and the yellow ridges of sand washed by the sea-waves seemed quivering. Chelkash started too. All at once Gavrilo tore himself from where he stood, flung himself at Chelkash's feet, threw his arms round them, and drew them toward him. Chelkash staggered; he sat heavily down on the sand, and grinding his teeth, brandished his long arm and clenched fist in the air. But before he had time to strike he was pulled up by Gavrilo's shame-faced and supplicating whisper:

"Friend! Give me—that money! Give it me, for Christ's sake! What is it to you? Why in one night— in only one night—while it would take me a year— Give it me—I will pray for you! Continually—in three churches—for the salvation of your soul! Why you'd cast it to the winds—while I'd put it into the land. O, give it me! Why, what does it mean to you? Did it cost you much? One night—and you're rich! Do a deed of mercy! You're a lost man, you see—you couldn't make your way—while I—oh, give it to me!"

Chelkash, dismayed, amazed, and wrathful, sat on the sand, thrown backward with his hands supporting him; he sat there in silence, rolling his eyes frightfully at the young peasant, who, ducking his head down at his knees, whispered his prayer to him in gasps. He shoved him away at last, jumped up to his feet, and thrusting his hands into his pockets, flung the rainbow notes at Gavrilo.

"There, cur! Swallow them!" he roared, shaking with excitement, with intense pity and hatred of this greedy slave. And as he flung him the money, he felt himself a hero. There was a reckless gleam in his eyes, an heroic air about his whole person.

"I'd meant to give you more, of myself. I felt sorry for you yesterday. I thought of the village. I thought: come, I'll help the lad. I was waiting to see what you'd do, whether you'd beg or not. While you!—Ah, you rag! you beggar! To be able—to torment oneself so—for money! You fool. Greedy devils! They're beside themselves—sell themselves for five kopecks! eh?"

"Dear friend! Christ have mercy on you! Why, what have I now! thousands!! I'm a rich man!" Gavrilo shrilled in ecstasy, all trembling, as he stowed away the notes in his bosom. "Ah, you good man! Never will I forget you! Never! And my wife and my children—I'll bid them pray for you!"

Chelkash listened to his shrieks and wails of ecstasy, looked at his radiant face that was contorted by greedy joy, and felt that he, thief and rake as he was, cast out from everything in life, would never be so covetous, so base, would never so forget himself. Never would he be like that! And this thought and feeling, filling him with a sense of his own independence and reckless daring, kept him beside Gavrilo on the desolate sea shore.

"You've made me happy!" shrieked Gavrilo, and snatching Chelkash's hand, he pressed it to his face.

Chelkash did not speak; he grinned like a wolf. Gavrilo still went on pouring out his heart:

"Do you know what I was thinking about? As we rowed here—I saw—the money—thinks I—I'll give it him—you—with the oar—one blow! the money's mine, and into the sea with him—you, that is—eh! Who'll miss him? said I. And if they do find him, they won't be inquisitive how—and who it was killed him. He's not a man, thinks I, that there'd be much fuss about! He's of no use in the world! Who'd stand up for him? No, indeed—eh?"

"Give the money here!" growled Chelkash, clutching Gavrilo by the throat.

Gavrilo struggled away once, twice. Chelkash's other arm twisted like a snake about him—there was the sound of a shirt tearing—and Gavrilo lay on the sand, with his eyes staring wildly, his fingers clutching at the air and his legs waving. Chelkash, erect, frigid, rapacious-looking, grinned maliciously, laughed a broken, biting laugh, and his mustaches twitched nervously in his sharp, angular face.

Never in all his life had he been so cruelly wounded, and never had he felt so vindictive.

"Well, are you happy now?" he asked Gavrilo through his laughter, and turning his back on him he walked away in the direction of the town. But he had hardly taken two steps when Gavrilo, crouched like a cat on one knee, and with a wide sweep of his arm, flung a round stone at him, viciously, shouting:

"O—one!"

Chelkash uttered a cry, clapped his hands to the nape of his neck, staggered forward, turned round to Gavrilo, and fell on his face on the sand. Gavrilo's heart failed him as he watched him. He saw him stir one leg, try to lift his head, and then stretch out, quivering like a bowsting. Then Gavrilo rushed fleeing away into the distance, where a shaggy black cloud hung over the foggy steppe, and it was dark. The waves whispered, racing up the sand, melting into it and racing back. The foam hissed and the spray floated in the air.

It began to rain, at first slightly, but soon a steady, heavy downpour was falling in streams from the sky, weaving a regular network of fine threads of water, that at once hid the steppe and the sea. Gavrilo vanished behind it. For a long while nothing was to be seen, but the rain and the long figure of the man stretched on the sand by the sea. But suddenly Gavrilo ran back out of the rain. Like a bird he flew up to Chelkash, dropped down beside him, and began to turn him over on the ground. His hand dipped into a warm, red stickiness. He shuddered and staggered back with a face pale and distraught.

"Brother, get up!" he whispered through the patter of the rain into Chelkash's ear.

Revived by the water on his face, Chelkash came to himself, and pushed Gavrilo away, saying hoarsely:

"Get—away!"

"Brother! Forgive me—it was the devil tempted me," Gavrilo whispered, faltering, as he kissed Chelkash's hand.

"Go along.   Get away!" he croaked.

"Take the sin from off my soul! Brother! Forgive me!"

"For—go away, do! Go to the devil!" Chelkash screamed suddenly, and he sat up on the sand. His face was pale and angry, his eyes were glazed, and kept closing, as though he were very sleepy. "What more—do you want? You've done—your job—and go away! Be off!" And he tried to kick Gavrilo away, as he knelt, overwhelmed, beside him, but he could not, and would have rolled over again if Gavrilo had not held him up, putting his arms round his shoulders. Chelkash's face was now on a level with Gavrilo's. Both were pale, piteous, and terrible-looking.

"Tfoo!" Chelkash spat into the wide, open eyes of his companion.

Meekly Gavrilo wiped his face with his sleeve, and murmured:

"Do as you will. I won't say a word. For Christ's sake, forgive me!"

"Snivelling idiot! Even stealing's more than you can do!" Chelkash cried scornfully, tearing a piece off his shirt under his jacket, and without a word, clenching his teeth now and then, he began binding up his head. "Did you take the notes?" he filtered through his teeth.

"I didn't touch them, brother! I didn't want them! there's ill-luck from them!"

Chelkash thrust his hand into his jacket pocket, drew out a bundle of notes, put one rainbow-colored note back in his pocket, and handed all the rest to Gavrilo.

"Take them and go!"

"I won't take them, brother. I can't! Forgive me!"

"T-take them, I say!" bellowed Chelkash, glaring horribly.

"Forgive me! Then I'll take them," said Gavrilo, timidly, and he fell at Chelkash's feet on the damp sand, that was being liberally drenched by the rain.

"You lie, you'll take them, sniveller!" Chelkash said with conviction, and with an effort, pulling Gavrilo's head up by the hair, he thrust the notes in his face.

"Take them! take them! You didn't do your job for nothing, I suppose. Take it, don't be frightened! Don't be ashamed of having nearly killed a man! For people like me, no one will make much inquiry. They'll say thank you, indeed, when they know of it. There, take it! No one will ever know what you've done, and it deserves a reward. Come, now!"

Gavrilo saw that Chelkash was laughing, and he felt relieved. He crushed the notes up tight in his hand.

"Brother! You forgive me? Won't you? Eh?" he asked tearfully.

"Brother of mine!" Chelkash mimicked him as he got, reeling, on to his legs. "What for? There's nothing to forgive. To-day you do for me, to-morrow I'll do for you."

"Oh, brother, brother!" Gavrilo sighed mournfully, shaking his head.

Chelkash stood facing him, he smiled strangely, and the rag on his head, growing gradually redder, began to look like a Turkish fez.

The rain streamed in bucketsful. The sea moaned

with a hollow sound. and the waves beat on the shore, lashing furiously and wrathfully against it.

The two men were silent.

"Come, good-bye!" Chelkash said, coldly and sarcastically.

He reeled, his legs shook, and he held his head queerly, as though he were afraid of losing it.

"Forgive me, brother!" Gavrilo besought him once more.

"All right!" Chelkash answered, coldly, setting off on his way.

He walked away, staggering, and still holding his head in his left hand, while he slowly tugged at his brown mustache with the right.

Gavrilo looked after him a long while, till the had disappeared in the rain, which still poured down in fine, countless streams, and wrapped everything in an impenetrable steel-gray mist.

Then Gavrilo took off his soaked cap, made the sign of the cross, looked at the notes crushed up in his hand, heaved a deep sigh of relief, thrust them into his bosom, and with long, firm strides went along the shore, in the opposite direction from that Chelkash had taken.

The sea howled, flinging heavy, breaking billows on the sand of the shore, and dashing them into spray, the rain lashed the water and the earth, the wind blustered. All the air was full of roaring, howling, moaning. Neither distance nor sky could be seen through the rain.

Soon the rain and the spray had washed away the red patch on the spot where Chelkash had lain, washed away the traces of Chelkash and the peasant lad on the sandy beach. And no trace was left on the seashore of the little drama that had been played out between two men.

MY FELLOW-TRAVELLER

(THE STORY OF A JOURNEY)

I MET him in the harbor of Odessa. For three successive days his square, strongly-built figure attracted my attention. His face—of a Caucasian type—was framed in a handsome beard. He haunted me. I saw him standing for hours together on the stone quay, with the handle of his walking stick in his mouth, staring down vacantly, with his black almond-shaped eyes, into the muddy waters of the harbor. Ten times a day, he would pass me by with the gait of a careless lounger. Whom could he be? I began to watch him. As if anxious to excite my curiosity, he seemed to cross my path more and more often. In the end, his fashionably-cut light check suit, his black hat, like that of an artist, his indolent lounge, and even his listless, bored glance grew quite familiar to me. His presence was utterly unaccountable, here in the harbor, where the whistling of the steamers and engines, the clanking of chains, the shouting of workmen, all the hurried maddening bustle of a port, dominated one's sensations, and deadened one's nerves and brain. Everyone else about the port was enmeshed in its immense complex machinery, which demanded incessant vigilance and endless toil. Everyone here was busy, loading and unloading either steamers or railway trucks. Everyone was tired and careworn. Everyone was hurrying to and fro, shouting or cursing, covered with dirt and sweat. In the midst of the toil and bustle this singular person, with his air of deadly boredom, strolled about deliberately, heedless of everything.

At last, on the fourth day, I came across him during the dinner hour, and I made up my mind to find out at any cost who he might be. I seated myself with my bread and water-melon not far from him, and began to eat, scrutinizing him and devising some suitable pretext for beginning a conversation with him.

There he stood, leaning against a pile of tea boxes, glancing aimlessly around, and drumming with his fingers on his walking stick, as if it were a flute. It was difficult for me, a man dressed like a tramp, with a porter's knot over my shoulders, and grimy with coal dust, to open up a conversation with such a dandy. But to my astonishment I noticed that he never took his eyes off me, and that an unpleasant, greedy, animal light shone in those eyes. I came to the conclusion that the object of my curiosity must be hungry, and after glancing rapidly round, I asked him in a low voice: "Are you hungry?"

He started, and with a famished grin showed rows of strong sound teeth. And he, too, looked suspiciously round. We were quite unobserved. Then I handed him half my melon and a chunk of wheaten bread. He snatched it all from my hand, and disappeared, squatting behind a pile of goods. His head peeped out from time to time; his hat was pushed back from his forehead, showing his dark moist brow. His face wore a broad smile, and for some unknown reason he kept winking at me, never for a moment ceasing to chew.

Making him a sign to wait a moment, I went away to buy meat, brought it, gave it to him, and stood by the boxes, thus completely shielding my poor dandy from outsiders' eyes. He was still eating ravenously, and constantly looking round as if afraid someone might snatch his food away; but after I returned, he began to eat more calmly, though still so fast and so greedily that it caused me pain to watch this famished man. And I turned my back on him.

"Thanks! Many thanks indeed!" He patted my shoulder, snatched my hand, pressed it, and shook it heartily.

Five minutes later he was telling me who he was. He was a Georgian prince, by name Shakro Ptadze, and was the only son of a rich landowner of Kutais in the Caucasus. He had held a position as clerk at one of the railway stations in his own country, and during that time had lived with a friend. But one fine day the friend disappeared, carrying off all the prince's money and valuables. Shakro determined to track and follow him, and having heard by chance that his late friend had taken a ticket to Batoum, he set off there. But in Batoum he found that his friend had gone on to Odessa. Then Prince Shakro borrowed a passport of another friend—a hair-dresser—of the same age as himself, though the features and distinguishing marks noted therein did not in the least resemble his own. Arrived at Odessa, he informed the police of his loss, and they promised to investigate the matter. He had been waiting for a fortnight, had consumed all his money, and for the last four days had not eaten a morsel.

I listened to his story, plentifully embellished as it was with oaths. He gave me the impression of being sincere. I looked at him, I believed him, and felt sorry for the lad. He was nothing more—he was nineteen, but from his naïvety one might have taken him for younger. Again and again, and with deep indignation, he returned to the thought of his close friendship for a man who had turned out to be a thief, and had stolen property of such value that Shakro's stern old father would certainly stab his son with a dagger if the property were not recovered.

I thought that if I didn't help this young fellow, the greedy town would suck him down. I knew through what trifling circumstances the army of tramps is recruited, and there seemed every possibility of Prince Shakro drifting into this respectable, but not respected class. I felt a wish to help him. My earnings were not sufficient to buy him a ticket to Batoum, so I visited some of the railway offices, and begged a free ticket for him. I produced weighty arguments in favor of assisting the young fellow, with the result of getting refusals just as weighty. I advised Shakro to apply to the Head of the Police of the town; this made him uneasy, and he declined to go there. Why not? He explained that he had not paid for his rooms at an hotel where he had been staying, and that when requested to do so, he had struck some one. This made him anxious to conceal his identity, for he supposed, and with reason, that if the police found him out he would have to account for the fact of his not paying his bill, and for having struck the man. Besides, he could not remember exactly if he had struck one or two blows, or more.

The position was growing more complicated.

I resolved to work till I had earned a sum sufficient to carry him back to Batoum. But alas! I soon realized that my plan could not be carried out quickly— by no means quickly—for my half-starved prince ate as much as three men, and more. At that time there was a great influx of peasants into the Crimea from the famine-stricken northern parts of Russia, and this had caused a great reduction in the wages of the workers at the docks. I succeeded in earning only eighty kopecks a day, and our food cost us sixty kopecks.

I had no intention of staying much longer at Odessa, for I had meant, some time before I came across the prince, to go on to the Crimea. I therefore suggested to him the following plan: that we should travel together on foot to the Crimea, and there I would find him another companion, who would continue the journey with him as far as Tiflis; if I should fail in finding him a fellow-traveler, I promised to go with him myself.

The prince glanced sadly at his elegant boots, his hat, his trousers, while he smoothed and patted his coat. He thought a little time, sighed frequently, and at last agreed. So we started off from Odessa to Tiflis on foot.

CHAPTER II.

By the time we had arrived at Kherson I knew something of my companion. He was a naïvely savage, exceedingly undeveloped young fellow; gay when he was well fed, dejected when he was hungry, like a strong, easy-tempered animal. On the road he gave me accounts of life in the Caucasus, and told me much about the landowners; about their amusements, and the way they treated the peasantry. His stories were interesting, and had a beauty of their own; but they produced on my mind a most unfavorable impression of the narrator himself.

To give one instance. There was at one time a rich prince, who had invited many friends to a feast. They partook freely of all kinds of Caucasian wines and meats, and after the feast the prince led his guests to his stables. They saddled the horses, the prince picked out the handsomest, and rode him into the fields. That was a fiery steed! The guests praised his form and paces. Once more the prince started to ride round the field, when at the same moment a peasant appeared, riding a splendid white horse, and overtook the prince —overtook him and laughed proudly! The prince was put to shame before his guests! He knit his brow, and beckoned the peasant to approach; then, with a blow of his dagger, he severed the man's head from his body. Drawing his pistol, he shot the white horse in the ear. He then delivered himself up to justice, and was condemned to penal servitude.

Through the whole story there rang a note of pity for

the prince. I endeavored to make Shakro understand that his pity was misplaced.

"There are not so many princes," he remarked didactically, "as there are peasants. It cannot be just to condemn a prince for a peasant. What, after all is a peasant? he is no better than this!" He took up a handful of soil, and added: "A prince is a star!"

We had a dispute over this question and he got angry. When angry, he showed his teeth like a wolf, and his features seemed to grow sharp and set.

"Maxime, you know nothing about life in the Caucasus; so you had better hold your tongue!" he shouted.

All my arguments were powerless to shatter his naïve convictions. What was clear to me seemed absurd to him. My arguments never reached his brain; but if ever I did succeed in showing him that my opinions were weightier and of more value than his own, he would simply say:

"Then go and live in the Caucasus, and you will see that I am right. What every one does *must* be right. Why am I to believe what you say? You are the only one who says such things are wrong; while thousands say they are right!"

Then I was silent, feeling that words were of no use in this case; only facts could confute a man, who believed that life, just as it is, is entirely just and lawful. I was silent, while he was triumphant, for he firmly believed that he knew life and considered his knowledge of it something unshakeable, stable and perfect. My silence seemed to him to give him a right to strike a fuller note in his stories of Caucasian life—a life full of so much wild beauty, so much fire and originality. These stories, though full of interest and attraction for me, continued to provoke my indignation and disgust by their cruelty, by the worship of wealth and of strength which they displayed, and the absence of that morality which is said to be binding on all men alike.

Once I asked him if he knew what Christ had taught.

"Yes, of course I do!" he replied, shrugging his shoulders.

But after I had examined him on this point, it turned out that all he knew was, that there had once been a certain Christ, who protested against the laws of the Jews, and that for this protest he was crucified by the Jews. But being a God, he did not die on the cross, but ascended into heaven, and gave the world a new law.

"What law was that?" I inquired.

He glanced at me with ironical incredulity, and asked: "Are you a Christian? Well, so am I a Christian. Nearly all the people in the world are Christians. Well, why do you ask then? You know the way they all live; they follow the law of Christ!"

I grew excited, and began eagerly to tell him about Christ's life. At first he listened attentively; but this attention did not last long, and he began to yawn.

I understood that it was useless appealing to his heart, and I once more addressed myself to his head, and talked to him of the advantages of mutual help and of knowledge, the benefits of obedience to the law, speaking of the policy of morality and nothing more.

"He who is strong is a law to himself! He has no

need of learning; even blind, he'll find his way," Prince
Shakro replied, languidly.

Yes, he was always true to himself. This made me
feel a respect for him; but he was savage and cruel, and
sometimes I felt a spark of hatred for Prince Shakro.
Still, I had not lost all hope of finding some point of
contact with him, some common ground on which we
could meet, and understand one another.

I began to use simpler language with the prince, and
tried to put myself mentally on a level with him. He
noticed these attempts of mine, but evidently mistaking
them for an acknowledgment on my part of his superiority, adopted a still more patronizing tone in talking
to me. I suffered, as the conviction came home to me,
that all my arguments were shattered against the stone
wall of his conception of life.

CHAPTER III.

Soon we had left Perekop behind us. We were approaching the Crimean mountains. For the last two
days we had seen them against the horizon. The mountains were pale blue, and looked like soft heaps of
billowy clouds. I admired them in the distance, and
I dreamed of the southern shore of the Crimea. The
prince hummed his Georgian songs and was gloomy.
We had spent all our money, and there was no chance
of earning anything in these parts.

We bent our steps toward Feodosia, where a new
harbor was in course of construction. The prince said
that he would work, too, and that when we had earned

enough money we would take a boat together to Batoum. In Batoum, he said, he had many friends, and
with their assistance he could easily get me a situation—
as a house-porter or a watchman. He clapped me pat-
ronizingly on the back, and remarked, indulgently, with
a peculiar click of his tongue:

"I'll arrange it for you! You shall have such a life!
tsé, tsé! You will have plenty of wine, there will be
as much mutton as you can eat. You can marry a
fat Georgian girl; tsé, tsé, tsé! She will cook you
Georgian dishes; give you children—many, many children! tsé, tsé, tsé!"

This constant repetition of "tsé, tsé, tsé!" surprised
me at first; then it began to irritate me, and, at last,
it reduced me to a melancholy frenzy. In Russia we
use this sound to call pigs, but in the Caucasus it seems
to be an expression of delight and of regret, of pleasure and of sadness.

Shakro's smart suit already began to look shabby;
his elegant boots had split in many places. His cane
and hat had been sold in Kherson. To replace the hat
he had bought an old uniform cap of a railway clerk.
When he put this cap on for the first time, he cocked
it on one side of his head, and asked: "Does it suit me?
Do I look nice?"

CHAPTER IV.

AT last we reached the Crimea. We had left Sim-
pheropol behind us, and were moving towards Jalta.

I was walking along in silent ectasy, marvelling at

the beauty of this strip of land, caressed on all sides by the sea.

The prince sighed, complained, and, casting dejected glances about him, tried filling his empty stomach with wild berries. His knowledge of their nutritive qualities was extremely limited, and his experiments were not always successful. Often he would remark, ill-humoredly:

"If I'm turned inside out with eating this stuff, how am I to go any farther? And what's to be done then?"

We had no chance of earning anything, neither had we a penny left to buy a bit of bread. All we had to live on was fruit, and our hopes for the future.

The prince began to reproach me with want of enterprise and laziness—with "gaping about," as he expressed it. Altogether, he was beginning to bore me; but what most tried my patience were his fabulous accounts of his appetite. According to these accounts, after a hearty breakfast at noon of roast lamb, and three bottles of wine, he could easily, at his two o'clock dinner, dispose of three plates of soup, a pot of pilave, a dish of shasleek, and various other Caucasian dishes, washed down abundantly with wine. For whole days he would talk of nothing but his gastronomic tastes and knowledge: and while thus talking, he would smack his lips, his eyes would glow, he would show his teeth, and grind them together; would suck in and swallow the saliva that came dripping from his eloquent lips. Watching him at these moments, I conceived for him a deep feeling of disgust, which I found difficult to conceal.

Near Jalta I obtained a job at clearing away the

dead branches in an orchard. I was paid fifty kopecks in advance, and laid out the whole of this money on bread and meat. No sooner had I returned with my purchase, than the gardener called me away to my work. I had to leave my store of food with Shakro, who, under the pretext of a headache, had declined to work. When I returned in an hour's time, I had to acknowledge that Shakro's stories of his appetite were all too true. Not a crumb was left of all the food I had bought! His action was anything but a friendly one, but I let it pass. Later on I had to acknowledge to myself the mistake I then made.

My silence did not pass unnoticed by Shakro, who profited by it in his own fashion. His behavior toward me from that time grew more and more shameless. I worked, while he ate and drank and urged me on, refusing, on various pretexts, to do any work himself. I am no follower of Tolstoi. I felt amused and sad as I saw this strong healthy lad watching me with greedy eyes when I returned from a hard day's labor, and found him waiting for me in some shady nook. But it was even more mortifying to see that he was sneering at me for working. He sneered at me because he had learned to beg, and because he looked on me as a lifeless dummy. When he first started begging, he was ashamed for me to see him, but he soon got over this; and as soon as we came to some Tartar village, he would openly prepare for business. Leaning heavily on his stick, he would drag one foot after him, as though he were lame. He knew quite well that the Tartars were mean, and never give alms to anyone who is strong and well. I argued with him, and tried to convince him of the shamefulness of such a course of action. He only sneered.

"I cannot work," was all he would reply.

He did not get much by his begging.

My health at that time began to give way. Every day the journey seemed to grow more trying. Every day our relations toward each other grew more strained. Shakro, now, had begun shamelessly to insist that I should provide him with food.

"It was you," he would say, "who brought me out here, all this way; so you must look after me. I never walked so far in my life before. I should never have undertaken such a journey on foot. It may kill me! You are tormenting me; you are crushing the life out of me! Think what it would be if I were to die! My mother would weep; my father would weep; all my friends would weep! Just think of all the tears that would be shed!"

I listened to such speeches, but was not angered by them. A strange thought began to stir in my mind, a thought that made me bear with him patiently. Many a time as he lay asleep by my side I would watch his calm, quiet face, and think to myself, as though groping after some idea:

"He is my fellow-traveller—my fellow-traveller."

At times, a dim thought would strike me, that after all Shakro was only right in claiming so freely, and with so much assurance, my help and my care. It proved that he possessed a strong will. He was enslaving me, and I submitted, and studied his character, following each quivering movement of the muscles of his face, trying to foresee when and at what point he would stop in this process of exploiting another person's individuality.

Shakro was in excellent spirits; he sang, and slept, and jeered at me, when he felt so disposed. Sometimes we separated for two or three days. I would leave him some bread and some money (if we had any), and would tell him where to meet me again. At parting, he would follow me with a suspicious, angry look in his eyes. But when we met again he welcomed me with gleeful triumph. He always said, laughing: "I thought you had run off alone, and left me! ha! ha! ha!" I brought him food, and told him of the beautiful places I had seen; and once even, speaking of Bakhtchesarai, I told him about our Russian poet Pushkin, and recited some of his verses. But this produced no effect on him.

"Oh, indeed; that is poetry, is it? Well, songs are better than poetry, I knew a Georgian once! *He* was the man to sing! He sang so loud—so loud—one would have thought his throat was being cut? He finished by murdering an inn-keeper, and was banished to Siberia."

Every time I returned, I sank lower and lower in the opinion of Shakro, until he could not conceal his contempt for me. Our position was anything but pleasant. I was seldom lucky enough to earn more than a rouble or a rouble and a-half a week, and I need not say that was not nearly sufficient to feed us both. The few bits of money that Shakro gained by begging made but little difference in the state of our affairs, for his belly was a bottomless pit, which swallowed everything that fell in its way; grapes, melons, salt fish, bread, or dried fruit; and as time went on he seemed to need ever more and more food.

Shakro began to urge me to hasten our departure from the Crimea, not unreasonably pointing out that autumn would soon be here and we had a long way still to go. I agreed with this view, and, besides, I had by then seen all that part of the Crimea. So we pushed on again toward Feodosia, hoping to earn something there. Once more our diet was reduced to fruit, and to hopes for the future.

Poor future! Such a load of hopes is cast on it by men, that it loses almost all its charms by the time it becomes the present!

When within some twenty versts of Aloushta we stopped, as usual, for our night's rest. I had persuaded Shakro to keep to the sea coast; it was a longer way round, but I longed to breathe the fresh sea breezes. We made a fire, and lay down beside it. The night was a glorious one. The dark green sea splashed against the rocks below; above us spread the majestic calm of the blue heavens, and around us sweet-scented trees and bushes rustled softly. The moon was rising, and the delicate tracery of the shadows, thrown by the tall, green plane trees, crept over the stones. Somewhere near a bird sang; its note was clear and bold. Its silvery trill seemed to melt into the air that was full of the soft, caressing splash of the waves. The silence that followed was broken by the nervous chirp of a cricket. The fire burned bright, and its flames looked like a large bunch of red and yellow flowers. Flickering shadows danced gaily around us, as if exulting in their power of movement, in contrast with the creeping advance of the moon shadows. From time to time strange sounds floated through the air. The broad expanse of sea horizon seemed lost in immensity. In the sky overhead not a cloud was visible. I felt as if I were lying on the earth's extreme edge, gazing into infinite space, that riddle that haunts the soul. The majestic beauty of the night intoxicated me, while my whole being seemed absorbed in the harmony of its colors, its sounds, and its scents.

A feeling of awe filled my soul, a feeling as if something great were very near to me. My heart throbbed with the joy of life.

Suddenly, Shakro burst into loud laughter, "Ha! ha! ha! How stupid your face does look! You've a regular sheep's head! Ha! ha! ha!"

I started as though it were a sudden clap of thunder. But it was worse. It was laughable, yes, but oh, how mortifying it was!

He, Shakro, laughed till the tears came. I was ready to cry, too, but from quite a different reason. A lump rose in my throat, and I could not speak. I gazed at him with wild eyes, and this only increased his mirth. He rolled on the ground, holding his sides. As for me, I could not get over the insult—for a bitter insult it was. Those—few, I hope—who will understand it, from having had a similar experience in their lives, will recall all the bitterness it left in their souls.

"Leave off!" I shouted, furiously.

He was startled and frightened, but he could not at once restrain his laughter. His eyes rolled, and his cheeks swelled as if about to burst. All at once he went off into a guffaw again. Then I rose and left him.

For some time I wandered about, heedless and almost unconscious of all that surrounded me, my whole soul consumed with the bitter pang of loneliness and of humiliation. Mentally, I had been embracing all nature. Silently, with the passionate love any man must feel if he has a little of the poet in him, I was loving and adoring her. And now it was nature that, under the form of Shakro, was mocking me for my passion. I might have gone still further in my accusations against nature, against Shakro, and against the whole of life, had I not been stopped by approaching footsteps.

"Do not be angry," said Shakro in a contrite voice, touching my shoulder lightly. "Were you praying? I didn't know it, for I never pray myself."

He spoke timidly, like a naughty child. In spite of my excitement, I could not help noticing his pitiful face ludicrously distorted by embarrassment and alarm.

"I will never interfere with you again. Truly! Never!" He shook his head emphatically. "I know you are a quiet fellow. You work hard, and do not force me to do the same. I used to wonder why; but, of course, it's because you are foolish as a sheep!"

That was his way of consoling me! That was his idea of asking for forgiveness! After such consolation, and such excuses, what was there left for me to do but forgive, not only for the past, but for the future!

Half an hour later he was sound asleep, while I sat beside him, watching him. During sleep, every one, be he ever so strong, looks helpless and weak, but Shakro looked a pitiful creature. His thick, half-parted lips, and his arched eyebrows, gave to his face a childish look of timidity and of wonder. His breathing was quiet and regular, though at times he moved restlessly, and muttered rapidly in the Georgian language; the words seemed those of entreaty. All around us reigned that intense calm which always makes one somehow expectant, and which, were it to last long, might drive one mad by its absolute stillness and the absence of sound —the vivid shadow of motion, for sound and motion seem ever allied.

The soft splash of the waves did not reach us. We were resting in a hollow gorge that was overgrown with bushes, and looked like the shaggy mouth of some petrified monster. I still watched Shakro, and thought: "This is my fellow traveler. I might leave him here, but I could never get away from him, or the like of him; their name is legion. This is my life companion. He will leave me only at death's door."

CHAPTER V.

At Feodosia we were sorely disappointed. All the work there was already apportioned among Turks, Greeks, Georgians, tramps, and Russian peasants from Poltava and Smolensk, who had all arrived before us. Already, more than four hundred men had, like ourselves, come in the hopes of finding employment; and were also, like ourselves, destined to remain silent spectators of the busy world going on in the port. In the town, and outside also, we met groups of famished peasants, gray and careworn, wandering miserably about. Of tramps there were also plenty, roving around like hungry wolves.

At first these tramps took us for famished peasants, and tried to make what they could out of us. They tore from Shakro's back the overcoat which I had bought him, and they snatched my knapsack from my shoulders. After several discussions, they recognized our intellectual and social kinship with them; and they returned us all our belongings. Tramps are men of honor, though they may be great rogues.

Seeing that there was no work for us, and that the construction of the harbor was going on very well without our help, we moved on resentfully toward Kertch.

My friend kept his word, and never again molested me; but he was terribly famished, his countenance was as black as thunder. He ground his teeth together, as does a wolf, whenever he saw someone else eating; and he terrified me by the marvellous accounts of the quantity of food he was prepared to consume. Of late he had begun to talk about women, at first only casually, with sighs of regret. But by degrees he came to talk more and more often on the subject, with the lascivious smile of "an Oriental." At length his state became such, that he could not see any person of the other sex, whatever her age or appearance, without letting fall some obscene remark about her looks or her figure. He spoke of women so freely, with so wide a knowledge of the sex; and his point of view, when discussing women, was so astoundingly direct, that his conversation filled me with disgust. Once I tried to prove to him that a woman was a being in no way inferior to him. I saw that he was not merely mortified by my words, but was on the point of violently resenting them as a personal insult. So I postponed my arguments till such time as Shakro should be well fed once more.

In order to shorten our road to Kertch we left the coast, and tramped across the steppes. There was nothing in my knapsack but a three-pound loaf of barley bread, which we had bought of a Tartar with our last five-kopeck piece. Owing to this painful circumstance, when, at last we reached Kertch, we could hardly move our legs, so seeking therefore work was out of the question. Shakro's attempts to beg by the way had proved unsuccessful; everywhere he had received the curt refusal: "There are so many of you."

This was only too true, for the number of people, who, during that bitter year, were in want of bread, was appalling. The famished peasants roamed about the country in groups, from three to twenty or more together. Some carried babies in their arms; some had young children dragging by the hand. The children looked almost transparent, with a bluish skin, under which flowed, instead of pure blood, some sort of thick unwholesome fluid. The way their small sharp bones projected from under the wasted flesh spoke more eloquently than could any words. The sight of them made one's heart ache, while a constant intolerable pain seemed to gnaw one's very soul.

These hungry, naked, worn-out children did not even cry. But they looked about them with sharp eyes that flashed greedily whenever they saw a garden, or a field, from which the corn had not yet been carried. Then they would glance sadly at their elders, as if asking "Why was I brought into this world?"

Sometimes they had a cart driven by a dried-up skeleton of an old woman, and full of children, whose little heads peeped out, gazing with mournful eyes in expressive silence at the new land into which they had been brought. The rough, bony horse dragged itself along, shaking its head and its tumbled mane wearily from side to side.

Following the cart, or clustering round it, came the grown-up people, with heads sunk low on their breasts, and arms hanging helplessly at their sides. Their dim, vacant eyes had not even the feverish glitter of hunger, but were full of an indescribable, impressive mournfulness. Cast out of their homes by misfortune, these processions of peasants moved silently, slowly, stealthily through the strange land, as if afraid that their presence might disturb the peace of the more fortunate inhabitants. Many and many a time we came across these processions, and every time they reminded me of a funeral without the corpse.

Sometimes, when they overtook us, or when we passed them, they would timidly and quietly ask us: "Is it much farther to the village?" And when we answered, they would sigh, and gaze dumbly at us. My travelling companion hated these irrepressible rivals for charity.

In spite of all the difficulties of the journey, and the

scantiness of our food, Shakro, with his rich vitality, could not acquire the lean, hungry look, of which the starving peasants could boast in its fullest perfection. Whenever he caught sight, in the distance, of these latter, he would exclaim: "Pouh! pouh! pouh. Here they are again! What are they roaming about for? They seem to be always on the move! Is Russia too small for them? I can't understand what they want! Russians are a stupid sort of people!"

When I had explained to him the reason of the "stupid" Russians coming to the Crimea, he shook his head incredulously, and remarked: "I don't understand! It's nonsense! We never have such 'stupid' things happening in Georgia!"

We arrived in Kertch, as I have said, exhausted and hungry. It was late. We had to spend the night under a bridge, which joined the harbor to the mainland. We thought it better to conceal ourselves, as we had been told that just before our arrival all the tramps had been driven out of the town. This made us feel anxious, lest we might fall into the hands of the police; besides Shakro had only a false passport, and if that fact became known, it might lead to serious complications in our future.

All night long the spray from the sea splashed over us. At dawn we left our hiding place, wet to the skin and bitterly cold. All day we wandered about the shore. All we succeeded in earning was a silver piece of the value of ten kopecks, which was given me by the wife of a priest, in return for helping her to carry home a bag of melons from the bazaar.

A narrow belt of water divided us from Taman, where we meant to go, but not one boatman would consent to carry us over in his boat, in spite of my pleadings. Everyone here was up in arms against the tramps, who, shortly before our arrival, had performed a series of heroic exploits; and we were looked upon, with good reason, as belonging to their set.

Evening came on. I felt angry with the whole world, for my lack of success; and I planned a somewhat risky scheme, which I put into execution as soon as night came on.

CHAPTER VI.

TOWARD evening, Shakro and I stole quietly up toward the boats of the custom house guardship. There were three of them, chained to iron rings, which rings were firmly screwed into the stone wall of the quay. It was pitch dark. A strong wind dashed the boats one against the other. The iron chains clanked noisily. In the darkness and the noise, it was easy for me to unscrew the ring from the stone wall.

Just above our heads the sentinel walked to and fro, whistling through his teeth a tune. Whenever he approached I stopped my work, though, as a matter of fact, this was a useless precaution; he could not even have suspected that a person would sit up to his neck in the water, at a spot where the backwash of a wave might at any moment carry him off his feet. Besides, the chains never ceased clanking, as the wind swung them backward and forward. Shakro was already lying full length along the bottom of the boat, muttering something, which the noise of the waves prevented me from hearing. At last the ring was in my hand. At the same moment a wave caught our boat, and dashed it suddenly some ten yards away from the side of the quay. I had to swim for a few seconds by the side of the boat, holding the chain in my hand. At last I managed to scramble in. We tore up two boards from the bottom, and using these as oars, I paddled away as fast as I could.

Clouds sailed rapidly over our heads; around, and underneath the boat, waves splashed furiously. Shakro sat aft. Every now and then I lost sight of him as the whole stern of the boat slipped into some deep watery gulf; the next moment he would rise high above my head, shouting desperately, and almost falling forward into my arms. I told him not to shout, but to fasten his feet to the seat of the boat, as I had already fastened mine. I feared his shouts might give the alarm. He obeyed, and grew so silent that I only knew he was in the boat by the white spot opposite to me, which I knew must be his face. The whole time he held the rudder in his hand; we could not change places, we dared not move.

From time to time I called out instructions as to the handling of the boat, and he understood me so quickly, and did everything so cleverly, that one might have thought he had been born a sailor. The boards I was using in the place of oars were of little use; they only blistered my hands. The furious gusts of wind served to carry the boat forward. I cared little for the direction, my only thought was to get the boat across to the other side. It was not difficult to steer, for the lights in Kertch were still visible, and served as a beacon. The waves splashed over our boat with angry hissings. The farther across we got, the more furious and the wilder became the waves. Already we could hear a sort of roar that held mind and soul as with a spell. Faster and faster our boat flew on before the wind, till it became almost impossible to steer a course. Every now and then we would sink into a gulf, and the next moment we would rise high on the summit of some enormous watery hill. The darkness was increasing, the clouds were sinking lower and lower. The lights of the town had disappeared.

Our state was growing desperate. It seemed as if the expanse of angry rollers was boundless and limitless. We could see nothing but these immense waves, that came rolling, one after another, out of the gloom, straight on to our boat. With an angry crash a board was torn from my hand, forcing me to throw the other into the boat, and to hold on tight with both hands to the gunwale. Every time the boat was thrown upward, Shakro shrieked wildly. As for me, I felt wretched and helpless, in the darkness, surrounded with angry waves, whose noise deafened me. I stared about me in dull and chilly terror, and saw the awful monotony around us. Waves, nothing but waves, with whitish crests, that broke in showers of salt spray; above us, the thick ragged edged clouds were like waves too.

I became conscious only of one thing: I felt that all that was going on around me might be immeasurably more majestic and more terrible, but that it did not deign to be, and was restraining its strength; and that I resented. Death is inevitable. But that impartial law, reducing all to the same commonplace level, seems to need something beautiful to compensate for its coarseness and cruelty. If I were asked to choose between a death by burning, or being suffocated in a dirty bog, I should choose the former; it is any way, a more seemly death.

"Let us rig up a sail," exclaimed Shakro.

"Where am I to find one?"

"Use my overcoat."

"Chuck it over to me then; but mind you don't drop the rudder into the water!"

Shakro quietly threw it to me. "Here! Catch hold!"

Crawling along the bottom of the boat, I succeeded in pulling up another board, one end of which I fixed into one of the sleeves of the coat. I then fixed the board against the seat, and held it there with my feet. I was just going to take hold of the other sleeve, when an unexpected thing happened. The boat was tossed suddenly upward, and then overturned. I felt myself in the water, holding the overcoat in one hand, and a rope, that was fastened to the boat, in the other hand. The waves swirled noisily over my head, and I swallowed a mouthful of bitter salt water. My nose, my mouth, and my ears, were full of it.

With all my might I clutched the rope, as the waves threw me backward and forward. Several times I sank, each time, as I rose again, bumping my head against the sides of the boat.

At last I succeeded in throwing the coat over the bottom of the boat, and tried to clamber on it myself. After a dozen efforts I scrambled up and I sat astride it. Then I caught sight of Shakro in the water on the opposite side of the boat, holding with both hands to the same rope of which I had just let go. The boat was apparently encircled by a rope, threaded through iron rings, driven into the outer planks.

"Alive!" I shouted.

At that moment Shakro was flung high into the air, and he, too, got on to the boat. I clutched him, and there we remained sitting face to face, astride on the capsized boat! I sat on it as though it were a horse, making use of the rope as if it had been stirrups; but our position there was anything but safe—a wave might easily have knocked us out of our saddle. Shakro held tightly by my knees, and dropped his head on my breast. He shivered, and I could hear his teeth chattering. Something had to be done. The bottom of the upturned boat was slippery, as though it had been greased with butter. I told Shakro to get into the water again, and hold by the ropes on one side of the boat, while I would do the same on the other side.

By way of reply, Shakro began to butt his head violently against my chest. The waves swept, in their wild dance, every now and then over us. We could hardly hold our seats; the rope was cutting my leg desperately. As far as one could see there was nothing but immense waves, rising mountains high, only to disappear again noisily.

I repeated my advice to Shakro in a tone of command. He fell to butting me more violently than ever. There was no time to be lost. Slowly and with difficulty I tore his hands from me, and began to push him into the water, trying to make his hands take hold of the rope. Then something happened that dismayed me more than anything in that terrible night.

"Are you drowning me?" he muttered, gazing at me.

This was really horrible! The question itself was a dreadful one, but the tone in which it was uttered more so. In it there was a timid submission to fate, and an entreaty for mercy, and the last sigh of one who had lost all hope of escaping from a frightful death. But more terrible still were the eyes that stared at me out of the wet, livid, death-like face.

"Hold on tighter!" I shouted to him, at the same time getting into the water myself, and taking hold of the rope. As I did so, I struck my foot against something, and for a moment I could not think for the pain. Then I understood. Suddenly a burning thought flashed through my mind. I felt delirious and stronger than ever.

"Land!" I shouted.

Great explorers may have shouted the word with more feeling on discovering new lands, but I doubt if any can have shouted more loudly. Shakro howled with delight, and we both rushed on in the water. But soon we both lost heart, for we were up to our chests in the waves, and still there seemed no sign of dry land. The waves were neither so strong nor so high, but they rolled slowly over our heads. Fortunately I had not let go of the boat, but still held on by the rope, which had already helped us when struggling in the water. Shakro and I moved carefully forward, towing the boat, which we had now righted, behind us.

Shakro was muttering and laughing. I glanced anxiously around. It was still dark. Behind us, and to our right, the roaring of the waves seemed to be increasing, whereas to our left and in front of us it was evidently growing less. We moved toward the left. The bottom was hard and sandy, but full of holes; sometimes we could not touch the bottom, and we had to take hold of the boat with one hand, while with the other hand, and our legs, we propelled it forward. At times again the water was no higher than our knees. When we came to the deep places Shakro howled, and I trembled with fear. Suddenly we saw ahead of us a light—we were safe!

Shakro shouted with all his might, but I could not forget that the boat was not ours, and promptly reminded him of the fact. He was silent, but a few minutes later I heard him sobbing. I could not quiet him —it was hopeless. But the water was gradually growing shallower, it reached our knees, then our ankles; and at last we felt dry land! We had dragged the boat so far, but our strength failed us, and we left it. A black log of wood lay across our path; we jumped over it, and stepped with our bare feet on to some prickly grass. It seemed unkind of the land to give us such a cruel welcome, but we did not heed it, and ran toward the fire. It was about a mile away; but it shone cheerily through the hovering gloom of the night, and seemed to smile a welcome to us.

CHAPTER VII.

THREE enormous shaggy dogs leaped up out of the darkness and ran toward us. Shakro, who had been sobbing all the way, now shrieked, and threw himself on the ground. I flung the wet overcoat at the dogs, and stooped down to find a stick or a stone. I could feel nothing but coarse, prickly grass, which hurt my hands. The dogs continued their attack. I put my fingers into my mouth, and whistled as loud as I could. They rushed back, and at the same time we heard the sound of approaching steps and voices.

A few minutes later, and we were comfortably seated around a fire in the company of four shepherds, dressed in "touloups" or long sheepskin overcoats.

They scrutinized us keenly and rather suspiciously, and remained silent all the time I was telling them our story.

Two of the shepherds were seated on the ground, smoking, and puffing from their mouths clouds of smoke. The third was a tall man with a thick black beard, wearing a high fur cap. He stood behind us, leaning on a huge knotted stick. The fourth man was younger, and fair haired; he was helping the sobbing Shakro to get off his wet clothes. An enormous stick, the size of which alone inspired fear, lay beside each of the seated shepherds.

Ten yards away from us all the steppe seemed covered with something gray and undulating, which had the appearance of snow in spring time, just when it is beginning to thaw. It was only after a close inspection that one could discern that this gray waving mass was composed of many thousands of sheep, huddled closely together, asleep, forming in the dark night one compact mass. Sometimes they bleated piteously and timidly.

I dried the overcoat by the fire, and told the shepherds all our story truthfully; even describing the way in which we became possessed of the boat.

"Where is that boat now?" inquired the severe-looking elder man, who kept his eyes fixed on me.

I told him.

"Go, Michael, and look for it."

Michael, the shepherd with the black beard, went off with his stick over his shoulder, toward the sea-shore.

The overcoat was dry. Shakro was about to put it on his naked body, when the old man said: "Go and have a run first to warm yourself. Run quickly around the fire. Come!"

At first, Shakro did not understand. Then suddenly he rose from his place, and began dancing some wild dance of his own, first flying like a ball across the fire, then whirling round and round in one place, then stamping his feet on the ground, while he swung his arms, and shouted at the top of his voice. It was a ludicrous spectacle. Two of the shepherds were rolling on the ground, convulsed with laughter, while the older man, with a serious, immovable face, tried to clap his hands in time to the dancing, but could not succeed in doing so. He watched attentively every movement of the dancing Shakro, while he nodded his head, and exclaimed in a deep bass voice:

"Hè! Hè! That's right! Hè! Hè!"

The light fell full on Shakro, showing the variety of his movements, as at one moment he would coil himself up like a snake, and the next would dance round on one leg; then would plunge into a succession of rapid steps, difficult to follow with the eye. His naked body shone in the fire light, while the large beads of sweat, as they rolled off it, looked, in the red light of the fire, like drops of blood.

By now, all three of the shepherds were clapping their hands; while I, shivering with cold, dried myself by the fire, and thought that our adventures would gratify the taste of admirers of Cooper or of Jules Vernes; there was shipwreck, then came hospitable aborigines, and a savage dance round the fire. And while I reflected thus, I felt very uneasy as to the chief point in every adventure—the end of it.

When Shakro had finished dancing, he also sat down by the fire, wrapped up in the overcoat. He was already eating, while he stared at me with his black eyes, which had a gleam in them of something I did not like. His clothes, stretched on sticks, driven into the ground, were drying before the fire. The shepherds had given me, also, some bread and bacon.

Michael returned, and sat down without a word beside the old man, who remarked in an inquiring voice: "Well?"

"I have found the boat," was the brief reply.

"It won't be washed away?"

"No."

The shepherds were silent, once more scrutinizing us.

"Well," said Michael, at last, addressing no one in particular. "Shall we take them to the ataman, or straight to the custom house officers?"

"So that's to be the end!" I thought to myself.

Nobody replied to Michael's question. Shakro went on quietly with his eating, and said nothing.

"We could take them to the ataman—or we could take them to the custom house. One plan's as good as the other," remarked the old man, after a short silence.

"They have stolen the custom house boat, so they ought to be taught a lesson for the future."

"Wait a bit, old man," I began.

"Certainly, they ought not to have stolen the boat. If they are not punished now, they will probably do something worse next time." The old man interrupted me, without paying any heed to my protestations.

The old man spoke with revolting indifference. When he had finished speaking, his comrades nodded their heads in token of assent.

"Yes, if a man steals, he has to bear the consequences, when he's caught—— Michael! what about the boat? Is it there?"

"Oh, it's there all right!"

"Are you sure the waves won't wash it away?"

"Quite sure."

"Well, that's all right. Then let it stay there. To-morrow the boatmen will be going over to Kertch, and they can take it with them. They will not mind taking an empty boat along with them, will they? Well—so you mean to say you were not frightened, you vagabonds? Weren't you indeed? La! la! la! Half a mile farther out, and you would have been by this time at the bottom of the sea! What would you have done if the waves had cast you back into the sea? Ay, sure enough, you would have sunk to the bottom like a couple of axes. And that would have been the end of you both!"

As the old man finished speaking, he looked at me with an ironical smile on his lips.

"Well, why don't you speak, lad?" he inquired.

I was vexed by his reflections, which I misinterpreted as sneering at us. So I only answered rather sharply:

"I was listening to you."

"Well—and what do you say?" inquired the old man.

"Nothing."

"Why are you rude to me? Is it the right thing to be rude to a man older than yourself?"

I was silent, acknowledging in my heart that it really was not the right thing.

"Won't you have something more to eat?" continued the old shepherd.

"No, I can't eat any more."

"Well, don't have any, if you don't want it. Perhaps you'll take a bit of bread with you to eat on the road?"

I trembled with joy, but would not betray my feelings.

"Oh, yes. I should like to take some with me for the road," I answered, quietly.

"I say, lads! give these fellows some bread and a piece of bacon each. If you can find something else, give it to them too."

"Are we to let them go, then?" asked Michael.

The other two shepherds looked up at the old man.

"What can they do here?"

"Did we not intend to take them either to the ataman or to the custom house?" asked Michael, in a dsappointed tone.

Shakro stirred uneasily in his seat near the fire, and poked out his head inquiringly from beneath the overcoat. He was quite serene.

"What would they do at the ataman's? I should think there is nothing to do there just now. Perhaps later on they might like to go there?"

"But how about the boat?" insisted Michael.

"What about the boat?" inquired the old man again. "Did you not say the boat was all right where it was?"

"Yes, it's all right there," Michael replied.

"Well, let it stay there. In the morning John can row it round into the harbor. From there, someone will get it over to Kertch. That's all we can do with the boat."

I watched attentively the old man's countenance, but failed to discover any emotion on his phlegmatic, sunburned, weather-beaten face, over the features of which the flicker from the flames played merrily.

"If only we don't get into trouble." Michael began to give way.

"There will be no trouble if you don't let your tongue wag. If the ataman should hear of it, we might get into a scrape, and they also. We have our work to do, and they have to be getting on. Is it far you have to go?" asked the old man again, though I had told him once before I was bound for Tiflis.

"That's a long way yet. The ataman might detain

them; then, when would they get to Tiflis? So let them be getting on their way. Eh?"

"Yes, let them go," all the shepherds agreed, as the old man, when he had finished speaking, closed his lips tightly, and cast an inquiring glance around him, as he fingered his gray beard.

"Well, my good fellows, be off, and God bless you!" he exclaimed with a gesture of dismissal. "We will see that the boat goes back, so don't trouble about that!"

"Many, many thanks, grandfather!" I said taking off my cap.

"What are you thanking me for?"

"Thank you; thank you!" I repeated fervently.

"What are you thanking me for? That's queer! I say, God bless you, and he thanks me! Were you afraid I'd send you to the devil, eh?"

"I'd done wrong and I was afraid," I answered.

"Oh!" and the old man lifted his eyebrows. "Why should I drive a man farther along the wrong path? I'd do better by helping one along the way I'm going myself. Maybe, we shall meet again, and then we'll meet as friends. We ought to help one another where we can. Good-bye!"

He took off his large shaggy sheepskin cap, and bowed low to us. His comrades bowed too.

We inquired our way to Anapa, and started off. Shakro was laughing at something or other.

CHAPTER VIII.

"WHY are you laughing?" I asked.

The old shepherd and his ethics of life had charmed

and delighted me. I felt refreshed by the pure air of early morning, blowing straight into my face. I rejoiced, as I watched the sky gradually clearing, and felt that daylight was not far off. Before long the morning sun would rise in a clear sky, and we could look forward to a brilliantly fine day.

Shakro winked slyly at me, and burst out into a fresh fit of laughter. The hearty, buoyant ring in his laugh made me smile also. The few hours rest we had taken by the side of the shepherd's fire, and their excellent bread and bacon, had helped us to forget our exhausting voyage. Our bones still ached a little, but that would pass off with walking.

"Well, what are you laughing at? Are you glad that you are alive? Alive and not even hungry?"

Shakro shook his head, nudged me in the ribs, made a grimace, burst out laughing again, and at last said in his broken Russian: "You don't see what it is that makes me laugh? Well, I'll tell you in a minute. Do you know what I should have done if we had been taken before the ataman? You don't know? I'd have told him that you had tried to drown me, and I should have begun to cry. Then they would have been sorry for me, and wouldn't have put me in prison! Do you see?"

At first I tried to make myself believe that it was a joke; but, alas! he succeeded in convincing me he meant it seriously. So clearly and completely did he convince me of it, that, instead of being furious with him for such naïve cynicism, I was filled with deep pity for him, and incidentally for myself as well. What else but pity can one feel for a man who tells one in all sincerity, with the brightest of smiles, of his intention to murder one? What is to be done with him if he looks upon such an action as a clever and delightful joke?

I began to argue warmly with him, trying to show him all the immorality of his scheme. He retorted very candidly that I did not see where his interests lay, and had forgotten he had a false passport and might get into trouble in consequence. Suddenly a cruel thought flashed through my mind.

"Stay," said I, "do you really believe that I wanted to drown you?"

"No! When you were pushing me into the water I did think so; but when you got in as well, then I didn't!"

"Thank God!" I exclaimed. "Well, thanks for that, anyway!"

"Oh! no, you needn't say thank you. I am the one to say thank you. Were we not both cold when we were sitting round the fire? The overcoat was yours, but you didn't take it yourself. You dried it, and gave it to me. And took nothing for yourself. Thank you for that! You are a good fellow; I can see that. When we get to Tiflis, I will reward you. I shall take you to my father. I shall say to him: 'Here is a man whom you must feed and care for, while I deserve only to be kept in the stable with the mules.' You shall live with us, and be our gardener, and we will give you wine in plenty, and anything you like to eat. Ah! you will have a capital time! You will share my wine and food!"

He continued for some time, describing in detail the attractions of the new life he was going to arrange for me in his home in Tiflis.

And as he talked, I mused on the great unhappiness of men equipped with new morality and new aspirations—they tread the paths of life lonely and astray; and the fellow-travelers they meet on the way are aliens to them, unable to understand them. Life is a heavy burden for these lonely souls. Helplessly they drift hither and thither. They are like the good seed, wafted in the air, and dropping but rarely onto fruitful soil.

Daylight had broken. The sea far away shone with rosy gold.

"I am sleepy," said Shakro.

We halted. He lay down in a trench, which the fierce gusts of wind had dug out in the dry sand, near the shore. He wrapped himself, head and all, in the overcoat, and was soon sound asleep. I sat beside him, gazing dreamily over the sea.

It was living its vast life, full of mighty movement.

The flocks of waves broke noisily on the shore and rippled over the sand, that faintly hissed as it soaked up the water. The foremost waves, crested with white foam, flung themselves with a loud boom on the shore, and retreated, driven back to meet the waves that were pushing forward to support them. Intermingling in the foam and spray, they rolled once more toward the shore, and beat upon it, struggling to enlarge the bounds of their realm. From the horizon to the shore, across the whole expanse of waters, these supple, mighty waves rose up, moving, ever moving, in a compact mass, bound together by the oneness of their aim. The sun shone more and more brightly on the crests of the breakers, which, in the distance on the horizon, looked blood-red. Not a drop went astray in the titanic heavings of the watery mass, impelled, it seemed, by some conscious aim, which it would soon attain by its vast rhythmic blows. Enchanting was the bold beauty of the foremost waves, as they dashed stubbornly upon the silent shore, and fine it was to see the whole sea, calm and united, the mighty sea, pressing on and ever on. The sea glittered now with all the colors of the rainbow, and seemed to take a proud, conscious delight in its own power and beauty.

A large steamer glided quietly round a point of land, cleaving the waters. Swaying majestically over the troubled sea, it dashed aside the threatening crests of the waves. At any other time this splendid, strong, flashing steamer would have set me thinking of the creative genius of man, who could thus enslave the elements. But now, beside me lay an untamed element in the shape of a man.

CHAPTER IX.

WE were tramping now through the district of Terek. Shakro was indescribably ragged and dishevelled. He was surly as the devil, though he had plenty of food now, for it was easy to find work in these parts. He himself was not good at any kind of work. Once he got a small job on a thrashing machine; his duty was to push aside the straw, as it left the machine; but after working half a day he left off, as the palms of his hands were blistered and sore. Another time he started off with me and some other workmen to root up trees, but he grazed his neck with a mattock.

We got on with our journey very slowly; we worked two days, and walked on the third day. Shakro ate all he could get hold of, and his gluttony prevented me from saving enough money to buy him new clothes. His ragged clothes were patched in the most fantastic way with pieces of various colors and sizes. I tried to persuade him to keep away from the beer houses in the villages, and to give up drinking his favorite wines; but he paid no heed to my words.

With great difficulty I had, unknown to him, saved up five roubles, to buy him some new clothes. One day, when we were stopping in some village, he stole the money from my knapsack, and came in the evening, in a tipsy state, to the garden where I was working. He brought with him a fat country wench, who greeted me with the following words: "Good-day, you damned heretic!"

Astonished at this epithet, I asked her why she called me a heretic. She answered boldly: "Because you forbid a young man to love women, you devil. How can you forbid what is allowed by law? Damn you, you devil!"

Shakro stood beside her, nodding his head approvingly. He was very tipsy, and he rocked backward and forward unsteadily on his legs. His lower lip drooped helplessly. His dim eyes stared at me with vacant obstinacy.

"Come, what are you looking at us for? Give him his money?" shouted the undaunted woman.

"What money?" I exclaimed, astonished.

"Give it back at once; or I'll take you before the ataman! Return the hundred and fifty roubles, which you borrowed from him in Odessa!"

What was I to do? The drunken creature might really go and complain to the Ataman; the Atamans were always very severe on any kind of tramp, and he might arrest us. Heaven only knew what trouble my arrest might inflict, not only on myself, but on Shakro! There was nothing for it but to try and outwit the woman, which was not, of course, a difficult matter.

She was pacified after she had disposed of three bottles of vodka. She sank heavily to the ground, on a bed of melons, and fell asleep. Then I put Shakro to sleep also.

Early next morning we turned our backs on the village, leaving the woman sound asleep among the melons.

After his bout of drunkenness, Shakro, looking far from well, and with a swollen, blotchy face, walked slowly along, every now and then spitting on one side, and sighing deeply. I tried to begin a conversation with him, but he did not respond. He shook his unkempt head, as does a tired horse.

It was a hot day; the air was full of heavy vapors, rising from the damp soil, where the thick, lush grass grew abundantly—almost as high as our heads. Around us, on all sides, stretched a motionless sea of velvety green grass. The hot air was steeped in strong sappy perfumes, which made one's head swim.

To shorten our way, we took a narrow path, where numbers of small red snakes glided about, coiling up under our feet. On the horizon to our right, were ranges of cloudy summits flashing silvery in the sun. It was the mountain chain of the Daguestan Hills.

The stillness that reigned made one feel drowsy, and plunged one into a sort of dreamy state. Dark, heavy clouds, rolling up behind us, swept slowly across the heavens. They gathered at our backs, and the sky there grew dark, while in front of us it still showed clear, except for a few fleecy cloudlets, racing merrily across the open. But the gathering clouds grew darker and swifter. In the distance could be heard the rattle of thunder, and its angry rumbling came every moment nearer. Large drops of rain fell, pattering on the grass, with a sound like the clang of metal. There was no place where we could take shelter. It had grown dark. The patter of the rain on the grass was louder still, but it had a frightened, timid sound. There was a clap of thunder, and the clouds shuddered in a blue flash of lightning. Again it was dark and the silvery chain of distant mountains was lost in the gloom. The rain now was falling in torrents, and one after another peals of thunder rumbled menacingly and incessantly over the vast steppe. The grass, beaten down by the wind and rain, lay flat on the ground, rustling faintly. Everything seemed quivering and troubled. Flashes of blinding lightning tore the storm clouds asunder. The silvery, cold chain of the distant mountains sprang up in the blue flash and gleamed with blue light. When the lightning died away, the mountains vanished, as though flung back into an abyss of darkness. The air was filled with rumblings and vibrations, with sounds and echoes. The lowering, angry sky seemed purifying itself by fire, from the dust and the foulness which had risen toward it from the earth, and the earth, it seemed, was quaking in terror at its wrath. Shakro was shaking and whimpering like a scared dog. But I felt elated and lifted above commonplace life as I watched the mighty, gloomy spectacle of the storm on the steppe. This unearthly chaos enchanted me and exalted me to an heroic mood, filling my soul with its wild, fierce harmony.

And I longed to take part in it, and to express, in some way or other, the rapture that filled my heart to overflowing, in the presence of the mysterious force which scatters gloom, and gathering clouds. The blue light which lit up the sky seemed to gleam in my soul too; and how was I to express my passion and my ecstasy at the grandeur of nature? I sang aloud, at the top of my voice. The thunder roared, the lightning flashed, the grass whispered, while I sang and felt myself in close kinship with nature's music. I was delirious, and it was pardonable, for it harmed no one but myself. I was filled with the desire to absorb, as much as possible, the mighty, living beauty and force that was raging on the steppe; and to get closer to it. A tempest at sea, and a thunderstorm on the steppes! I know nothing grander in nature. And so I shouted to my heart's content, in the absolute belief that I troubled no one, nor placed any one in a position to criticize my action. But suddenly, I felt my legs seized, and I fell helpless into a pool of water.

Shakro was looking into my face with serious and wrathful eyes.

"Are you mad? Aren't you? No? Well, then, be quiet! Don't shout! I'll cut your throat! Do you understand?"

I was amazed, and I asked him first what harm I was doing him?

"Why, you're frightening me! It's thundering; God is speaking, and you bawl. What are you thinking about?"

I replied that I had a right to sing whenever I chose. Just as he had.

"But I don't want to!" he said.

"Well, don't sing then!" I assented.

"And don't you sing!" insisted Shakro.

"Yes, I mean to sing!"

"Stop! What are you thinking about?" he went on angrily. "Who are you? You have neither home nor father, nor mother; you have no relations, no land! Who are you? Are you anybody, do you suppose? It's I am somebody in the world! I have everything!"

He slapped his chest vehemently.

"I'm a prince, and you—you're nobody—nothing! You say—you're this and that! Who else says so? All Koutais and Tiflies know me! You shall not contradict me! Do you hear? Are you not my servant? I'll pay ten times over for all you have done for me. You *shall* obey me! You said yourself that God taught us to serve each other without seeking for a reward; but I'll reward you.

"Why will you annoy me, preaching to me, and frightening me? Do you want me to be like you? That's too bad! You can't make me like yourself! Foo! Foo!"

He talked, smacked his lips, snuffled, and sighed. I stood staring at him, open-mouthed with astonishment. He was evidently pouring out now all the discontent, displeasure and disgust, which had been gathering up during the whole of our journey. To convince me more thoroughly, he poked me in the chest from time to time with his forefinger, and shook me by the shoulder. During the most impressive parts of his speech he pushed up against me with his whole massive body. The rain was pouring down on us, the thunder never ceased its muttering, and to make me hear, Shakro shouted at the top of his voice. The tragic comedy of my position struck me more vividly than ever, and I burst into a wild fit of laughter. Shakro turned away and spat.

CHAPTER X

THE nearer we draw to Tiflis, the gloomier and the surlier grew Shakro. His thinner, but still stolid face wore a new expression. Just before we reached Vladikavkas we passed through a Circassian village, where we obtained work in some maize fields.

The Circassians spoke very little Russian, and as they constantly laughed at us, and scolded us in their own language, we resolved to leave the village two days after our arrival; their increasing enmity had begun to alarm us.

We had left the village about ten miles behind, when Shakro produced from his shirt a roll of home-spun muslin, and handing it to me, exclaimed triumphantly: "You need not work any more now. We can sell this, and buy all we want till we get to Tiflis! Do you see?"

I was moved to fury, and tearing the bundle from his hands, I flung it away, glancing back.

The Circassians are not to be trifled with! Only a short time before, the Cossacks had told us the following story:

A tramp, who had been working for some time in a Circassian village, stole an iron spoon, and carried it away with him. The Circassians followed him, searched him, and found the iron spoon. They ripped open his body with a dagger, and after pushing the iron spoon into the wound, went off quietly, leaving him to his fate on the steppes. He was found by some Cossacks at the point of death. He told them this story, and died on the way to their village. The Cossacks had more than once warned us against the Circassians, relating many other edifying tales of the same sort. I had no reason to doubt the accuracy of these stories. I reminded Shakro of these facts. For some time he listened in silence to what I was saying; then, suddenly, showing his teeth and screwing up his eyes, he flew at me like a wild cat. We struggled for five minutes or so, till Shakro exclaimed angrily: "Enough! Enough!"

Exhausted with the struggle, we sat in silence for some time, facing each other. Shakro glanced covetously toward the spot, where I had flung the red muslin, and said:

"What were we fighting about? Fa—Fa—Fa! It's very stupid. I did not steal it from *you*, did I? Why should you care? I was sorry for you that is why I took the linen. You have to work so hard, and I cannot help you in that way, so I thought I would help you by stealing. Tsè! Tsè!

I made an attempt to explain to him how wrong it was to steal.

"Hold your tongue, please! You're a blockhead!" he exclaimed contemptuously; then added: "When one is dying of hunger, there is nothing for it but to steal; what sort of a life is this?"

I was silent, afraid of rousing his anger again. This was the second time he had committed a theft. Some time before, when we were tramping along the shores of the Black Sea, he stole a watch belonging to a fisherman. We had nearly come to blows then.

"Well, come along," he said; when, after a short rest, we had once more grown quiet and friendly.

So we trudged on. Each day made him grow more gloomy, and he looked at me strangely, from under his brows.

As we walked over the Darial Pass, he remarked: "Another day or two will bring us to Tiflis. Tsè! Tsè!"

He clicked his tongue, and his face beamed with delight.

"When I get home, they will ask me where I have been? I shall tell them I have been travelling. The first thing I shall do will be to take a nice bath. I shall eat a lot. Oh! what a lot. I have only to tell my mother 'I am hungry!' My father will forgive when I tell him how much trouble and sorrow I have undergone. Tramps are a good sort of people! Whenever I meet a tramp, I shall always give him a rouble, and take him to the beer-house, and treat him to some wine. I shall tell him I was a tramp myself once. I shall tell my father all about you. I shall say: 'This man—he was like an elder brother to me. He lectured me, and beat me, the dog! He fed me, and now, I shall say, you must feed him.' I shall tell him to feed you for a whole year. Do you hear that, Maxime?"

I liked to hear him talk in this strain; at those times he seemed so simple, so child-like. His words were all the more pleasant because I had not a single friend in all Tiflis. Winter was approaching. We had already been caught in a snowstorm in the Goudaour hills. I reckoned somewhat on Shakro's promises. We walked on rapidly till we reached Mesket, the ancient capital of Iberia. The next day we hoped to be in Tiflis.

I caught sight of the capital of the Caucasus in the distance, as it lay some five versts farther on, nestling between two high hills. The end of our journey was fast approaching! I was rejoicing, but Shakro was indifferent. With a vacant look he fixed his eyes on the distance, and began spitting on one side; while he kept rubbing his stomach with a grimace of pain. The pain in his stomach was caused by his having eaten too many raw carrots, which he had pulled up by the wayside.

"Do you think I, a nobleman of Georgia, will show myself in my native town, torn and dirty as I am now? No, indeed, that I never could! We must wait outside till night. Let us rest here."

We twisted up a couple of cigarettes from our last bit of tobacco, and, shivering with cold, we sat down under the walls of a deserted building to have a smoke. The piercing cold wind seemed to cut through our bodies. Shakro sat humming a melancholy song; while I fell to picturing to myself a warm room, and other advantages of a settled life over a wandering existence.

"Let us move on now!" said Shakro resolutely.

It had now become dark. The lights were twinkling down below in the town. It was a pretty sight to watch them flashing one after the other, out of the mist of the valley, where the town lay hidden.

"Look here, you give me your bashleek,* I want to cover my face up with it. My friends might recognize me."

I gave him my bashleek. We were already in Olga Street, and Shakro was whistling boldly.

"Maxime, do you see that bridge over yonder? The tram stops there. Go and wait for me there, please. I want first to go and ask a friend, who lives close by; about my father and mother."

"You won't be long, will you?"

"Only a minute. Not more!"

---

* A kind of hood worn by men to keep their ears warm.

He plunged rapidly down the nearest dark, narrow lane, and disappeared—disappeared for ever.

I never met him again—the man who was my fellow-traveller for nearly four long months; but I often think of him with a good-humored feeling, and light-hearted laughter.

He taught me much that one does not find in the thick volumes of wise philosophers, for the wisdom of life is always deeper and wider than the wisdom of men.

ON A RAFT

HEAVY clouds drift slowly across the sleepy river and hang every moment lower and thicker. In the distance their ragged gray edges seem almost to touch the surface of the rapid and muddy waters, swollen by the floods of spring, and there, where they touch, an impenetrable wall rises to the skies, barring the flow of the river and the passage of the raft.

The stream, swirling against this wall—washing vainly against it with a wistful wailing swish—seems to be thrown back on itself, and then to hasten away on either side, where lies the moist fog of a dark spring night.

The raft floats onward, and the distance opens out before it into heavy cloud—massed space. The banks of the rivers are invisible; darkness covers them, and the lapping waves of a spring flood seem to have washed them into space.

The river below has spread into a sea; while the

heavens above, swatched in cloud masses, hang heavy, humid, and leaden.*

There is no atmosphere, no color in this gray blurred picture.

The raft glides down swiftly and noiselessly, while out of the darkness appears, suddenly bearing down on it, a steamer, pouring from its funnels a merry crowd of sparks, and churning up the water with the paddles of its great revolving wheels.

The two red forward lights gleam every moment larger and brighter, and the mast-head lantern sways slowly from side to side, as if winking mysteriously at the night. The distance is filled with the noise of the troubled water, and the heavy thud-thud of the engines.

"Look ahead!" is heard from the raft. The voice is that of a deep-chested man.

Two men are standing aft, grasping each a long pole, which propel the raft and act as rudders; Mitia, the son

---

* The river is the Volga, and the passage of strings of rafts down its stream in early spring is being described by the author. The allusion later on to the Brotherhood living in the Caucasus, refers to the persecuted Doukhobori, who have since been driven from their homes by the Russian authorities and have taken refuge in Canada.

In order to enter into the sociology of this story of Gorky's it must be explained that among ancient Russian folk-customs, as the young peasants were married at a very early age, the father of the bridegroom considered he had rights over his daughter-in-law. In later times, this custom, although occasionally continued, was held in disrepute among the peasantry; but that it has not entirely died out is proved by the little drama sketched in by the hand of a genius in "On a Raft."

of the owner, a fair, weak, melancholy-looking lad of
twenty-two; and Sergei, a peasant, hired to help in the
work on board the raft, a bluff, healthy, red-bearded fellow, whose upper lip, raised with a mocking sneer, dis-
closes a mouth filled with large, strong teeth.

"Starboard!" A second cry vibrates through the
darkness ahead of the rafts.

"What are you shouting for; we know our business!"
Sergei growls raspingly; pressing his expanded chest
against the pole. "Ouch! Pull harder, Mitia!" Mitia
pushes with his feet against the damp planks that form
the raft, and with his thin hands draws toward him the
heavy steering pole, coughing hoarsely the while.

"Harder, to starboard! You cursed loafers!" The
master cries again, anger and anxiety in his voice.

"Shout away!" mutters Sergei. "Here's your miserable devil of a son, who couldn't break a straw across
his knee, and you put him to steer a raft; and then
you yell so that all the river hears you. You were
mean enough not to take a second steersman; so now
you may tear your throat to pieces shouting!"

These last words were growled out loud enough to
be heard forward, and as if Sergei wished they should
be heard.

The steamer passed rapidly alongside the raft sweep-
ing the frothing water from under her paddle wheels.
The planks tossed up and down in the wash, and the
osier branches fastening them together, groaned and
scraped with a moist, plaintive sound.

The lit-up portholes of the steamer seem for a moment to rake the raft and the river with fiery eyes, re-

flected in the seething water, like luminous trembling
spots.   Then all disappears.

The wash of the steamer sweeps backward and forward, over the raft; the planks dance up and down.
Mitia, swaying with the movements of the water,
clutches convulsively the steering pole to save himself
from falling.

"Well, well," says Sergei, laughing,   "So you're beginning to dance! Your father will start yelling again.
Or he'll perhaps come and give you one or two in the
ribs; then you'll dance to another tune!   Port side
now!   Ouch!"

And with his muscles strung like steel springs,
Sergei gives a powerful push to his pole, forcing it
deep down into the water.   Energetic, tall, mocking
and rather malicious, he stands bare-footed, rigid, as
if a part of the planks; looking straight ahead, ready
at any moment to change the direction of the raft.

"Just look there at your father kissing Marka!
Aren't they a pair of devils? No shame, and no conscience. Why don't you get away from them, Mitia
—away from these Pagan pigs? Why? Do you
hear?"

"I hear," answered Mitia in a stifled voice, without
looking toward the spot which Sergei pointed to
through the darkness, where the form of Mitia's father
could be seen.

"I hear," mocked Sergei, laughing ironically.

"You poor half-baked creature! A pleasant state of
things indeed!" he continued, encouraged by the apathy
of Mitia. "And what a devil that old man is! He

finds a wife for his son; he takes the son's wife away from him; and all's well! The old brute!"

Mitia is silent, and looks astern up the river, where another wall of mist is formed. Now the clouds close in all round, and the raft hardly appears to move, but to be standing still in the thick, dark water, crushed down by the heavy gray-black vaporous masses, which drift across the heavens, and bar the way.

The whole river seems like a fathomless, hidden whirlpool, surrounded by immense mountains, rising toward heaven, and capped with shrouding mists.

The stillness suffocates, and the water seems spellbound with expectation, as it beats softly against the raft. A great sadness, and a timid questioning is heard in that faint sound—the only voice of the night—accentuating still more the silence. "We want a little wind now," says Sergei. "No it's not exactly wind we want—that would bring rain," he replies to himself, as he begins to fill his pipe. A match strikes, and the bubbling sound of a pipe being lighted is heard. A red gleam appears, throwing a glow over the big face of Sergei; and then, as the light dies down he is lost in the darkness.

"Mitia!" he cries. His voice is now less brutal and more mocking.

"What is it?" replies Mitia, without moving his gaze from the distance, where he seems with his big sad eyes to be searching for something.

"How did it happen, mate? How did it happen?"

"What?" answers Mitia, displeased.

"How did you come to marry? What a queer set out!

How was it? You brought your wife home!—and then? Ha! ha! ha!"

"What are you cackling about? Look out there!" came threateningly across the river.

"Damned beast!" ejaculates with delight Sergei; and returns to the theme that interests him. "Come, Mitia; tell me; tell me at once—why not?"

"Leave me alone, Sergei," Mitia murmurs entreatingly; "I told you once."

But knowing by experience that Sergei will not leave him in peace, he begins hurriedly: "Well, I brought her home—and I told her: 'I can't be your husband, Marka; you are a strong girl, and I am a feeble, sick man. I didn't wish at all to marry you, but my father would force me to marry.' He was always saying to me, 'Get married! Get married!' I don't like women, I said: and you especially, you are too bold. Yes—and I can't have anything to do—with it. Do you understand? For me, it disgusts me, and it is a sin. And children—one is answerable to God for one's children."

"Disgusts," yells Sergei and laughs. "Well! and what did Marka reply? What?"

"She said, 'What shall I do now?' and then she began to cry. 'What have you got against me? Am I so dreadfully ugly?' She is shameless, Sergei, and wicked! 'With all this health and strength of mine, must I go to my father-in-law?' And I answered: 'If you like— go where you wish, but I can't act against my soul. If I had love for you, well and good; but being as it is, how is it possible? Father Ivan says it's the deadliest sin. We are not beasts, are we?' She went on crying:

'You have ruined my chances in life!' And I pitied her very much. 'It's nothing,' I said; 'things will come all right. Or,' I continued, 'you can go into a convent.' And she began to insult me. 'You are a stupid fool, Mitia!—a coward!'"

"Well, I'm blest!" exclaims Sergei, in a delighted whisper. "So you told her straight to go into a convent?"

"Yes, I told her to go," answers Mitia simply.

"And she told you you were a fool?" queried Sergei, raising his voice.

"Yes, she insulted me."

"And she was right, my friend; yes, indeed, she was right! You deserve a proper hammering." And Sergei, changing suddenly his tone, continued with severity and authority: "Have you any right to go against the law? But you *did* go against it! Things are arranged in a certain way, and it's no use going against them! You mustn't even discuss them. But what did you do? You got some maggot into your head. A convent, indeed! Silly fool! What did the girl want? Did she want your convent? What a set of muddle-headed fools there seems to be now! Just think what's happened! *You*, you're neither fish nor fowl, nor good red-herring. And the girl's done for! She's living with an old man! And you drove the old man into sin! How many laws have *you* broken? You clever head!"

"Law, Sergei, is in the soul. There is one law for everyone. Don't do things that are against your soul, and you will do no evil on the earth," answered Mitia, in a slow, conciliatory tone, and nodding his head.

"But you did do evil," answered Sergei, energetically. "In the soul! A fine idea! There are many things in the soul. Certain things *must* be forbidden. The soul, the soul! You must first understand it, my friend, and then——"

"No, it's not so, Sergei," replied Mitia with warmth, and he seemed to be inspired. "The soul, my friend, is always as clear as dew. It's true, its voice lies deep down within us, and is difficult to hear: but if we listen, we can never be mistaken. If we act according to what is in our soul, we shall always act according to the will of God. God is in the soul, and, therefore, the law must be in it. The soul was created by God, and breathed by God into man. We have only to learn to look into it— and we must look into it without sparing our own feelings."

"You sleepy devils! Look ahead there!" The voice thundered from the forward part of the raft, and swept back down the river. In the strength of the sound one could recognize that the owner of the voice was healthy, energetic, and pleased with himself. A man with large and conscious vitality. He shouted, not because he had to give a necessary order to the steersmen, but because his soul was full of life and strength, and this life and strength wanted to find free expression, so it rushed forth in that thunderous and forceful sound.

"Listen to the old blackguard shouting," continued Sergei with delight, looking ahead with a piercing glance, and smiling. "Look at them billing and cooing like a pair of doves! Don't you ever envy them, Mitia?"

Mitia watched with indifference the working of the

two forward oars, held by two figures who moved backward and forward, forming sometimes as they touched each other one compact and dark mass.

"So you say you don't envy them?" repeated Sergei.

"What is it to me? It's their sin, and they must answer for it," replied Mitia quietly.

"Hm!" ironically interjected Sergei, while he filled his pipe.

Once more the small red patch of light glowed in the darkness; and the night grew thicker, and the gray clouds sank lower toward the swollen river.

"Where did you get hold of that fine stuff, or does it come to you naturally? But you don't take after your father, my lad! Your father's a fine old chap. Look at him! He's fifty-two now, and see what a strapping wench he's carrying on with! She's as fine a woman as ever wore shoe-leather. And she loves him; it's no use denying it! She loves him, my lad! One can't help admiring him, he's such a trump, your father—he's the king of trumps! When he's at work, it's worth while watching him. And then, he's rich! And then, look how he's respected! And his head's screwed on the right way. Yes. And you? You're not a bit like either your father or your mother? What would your father have done, Mitia, do you think, if old Anfisa had lived? That would have been a good joke! I should have liked to have seen how she's have settled him! She was the right sort of woman, your mother! a real plucky one, she was! They were well matched!"

Mitia remained silent, leaning on the pole, and staring at the water.

Sergeï ceased talking. Forward on the raft was heard a woman's shrill laugh, followed by the deeper laugh of a man. Their figures, blurred by the mist, were nearly invisible to Sergei, who, however, watched them curiously. The man appeared as a tall figure, standing with legs wide apart, holding a pole, and half turned toward a shorter woman's figure, leaning on another pole, and standing a few paces away. She shook her forefinger at the man, and giggled provokingly.

Sergei turned away his head with a sigh, and after a few moment's silence began to speak again.

"Confound it all, but how jolly they seem together; it's good to see! Why can't I have something like that? I, a waif and a stray! I'd never leave such a woman! I'd always have my arms round her, and there'd be no mistake about *my* loving the little devil! I've never had any luck with women! They don't like ginger hair— women don't. No. She's a woman with fancies, she is! She's a sly little devil! She wants to see life! Are you asleep, Mitia?"

"No," answered Mitia quietly.

"Well, how are you going to live? To tell the truth, you're as solitary as a post! That seems pretty hard! Where can you go? You can't earn your living among strangers. You're too absurd! What's the use of a man who can't stand up for himself? A man's got to have teeth and claws in this world! They'll all have a go at you. Can you stick up for yourself? How would you set about it? Damn it all; where the devil *could* you go?"

"I," said Mitia, suddenly arousing herself; "I shall go

away. I shall go in the autumn to the Caucasian Mountains, and that will be the end of it all. My God! If only I could get away from you all! Soulless, godless men! To get away from you, that's my only hope! What do you live for? Where is your God? He's nothing but a name! Do you live in Christ? You are wolves; that's what you are! But over there live other men, whose souls live in Christ. Their hearts contain love, and they are athirst for the salvation of the world. But you—you are beasts, spewing out filth. But other men there are; I have seen them; they called me, and I must go to them. They gave me the book of Holy Writ, and they said: 'Read, man of God, our beloved brother, read the word of truth!' And I read, and my soul was renewed by the word of God. I shall go away. I shall leave all you ravening wolves. You are rending each other's flesh! Accursed be ye!"

Mitia spoke in a passionate whisper, as if overpowered by the intensity of his contemplative rapture, his anger with the ravening wolves, and his desire to be with those other men, whose souls aspired toward the salvation of the world. Sergei was taken aback. He remained quiet for some time, open-mouthed, holding his pipe in his hand. After a few moments' thought he glanced round, and said in a deep, rough voice: "Damn it all! Why you're turned a bad 'un all at once! Why did you read that book? It was very likely an evil one. Well, be off, be off! If not, there'll be an end of you! Be off with you before you become a regular beast yourself! And who are these fellows in the Caucasus? Monks? Or what?"

But the fire of Mitia's spirit died down as quickly as it had been kindled to a flame; he gasped with the exertion as he worked the pole, and muttered to himself below his breath.

Sergei waited some time for the answer which did not come. His simple, hardy nature was quelled by the grim and death-like stillness of the night. He wanted to recall the fullness of life, to wake the solitude with sound, to disturb and trouble the hidden meditative silence of the leaden mass of water, flowing slowly to the sea; and of the dull, threatening clouds hanging motionless in the air. At the other end of the raft there was life, and it called on him to live.

Forward, he could hear every now and then bursts of contented laughter, exclamations, sounds that seemed to stand out against the silence of this night, laden with the breath of spring, and provoking such passionate life desires.

"Hold hard, Mitia! you'll catch it again from the old man! Look out there!" said Sergei, who could not stand the silence any longer; and watching Mitia, who aimlessly moved his pole backward and forward in the water.

Mitia, wiping his moist brow, stood quietly leaning with his breast against the pole, and panting.

"There are few steamers to-night," continued Sergei; "we've only passed one these many hours." Seeing that Mitia had no intention of answering, Sergei replied quietly to himself: "It's because its too early in the season. It's only just beginning. We shall soon be at Kazan. The Volga pulls hard. She has a mighty strong back, that can carry all. Why are you standing still like that? Are you angry? Hi, there, Mitia!"

"What's the matter?" Mitia cried in a vexed tone.

"Nothing, you strange fellow; but why can't you talk? You are always thinking. Leave it alone! Thinking is bad for a man. A wise sort of fellow you are! You think and think, and all the time you can't understand that you're a fool at bottom. Ha! Ha!"

And Sergei, very well satisfied with his own superiority, cleared his throat, remained quiet for a moment, whistled a note, and then continued to develop his theme.

"Thinking? Is that an occupation for a working man? Look at your father; he doesn't think much; he lives. He loves your wife, and they laugh at you together; you wise fool! That's about it! Just listen to them! Blast them! I believe Marka's already with child. Never fear, the child won't feature you. He'll be a fine, lusty lad, like Silan himself! But he'll be *your* child! Ha! Ha! Ha! He'll call *you* father! And you won't be his father, but his brother; and his real father will be his grandfather! That's a nice state of things! What a filthy family! But they're a strapping pair! Isn't that true, Mitia?"

"Sergei!" In a passionate, sobbing whisper. "In the name of Christ I entreat you don't tear my soul to pieces, don't brand me with fire. Leave me alone. Do be quiet! In the name of God and of Christ, I beg you not to speak to me! Don't disturb me! Don't drain my heart's blood! I'll throw myself in the river, and yours will be the sin, and a great sin it will be! I should lose my soul; don't force me to it! For God's sake, I entreat you!"

The silence of the night was troubled with shrill, un-natural sobbing; and Mitia fell on the deck of the raft, as if a blast from the overhanging clouds had struck him down.

"Come, come!" growled Sergei, anxiously watching his mate writhing on the deck, as if scorched with fire. "What a strange man! He ought to have told me if it was not—if it was not quite——"

"You've been torturing me all the way. Why? Am I your enemy?" Mitia sobbed again.

"You're a strange lad! a rum un!" murmured Sergei, confused and offended. "How could I know? I couldn't tell you'd take on like that!"

"Understand, then, that I want to forget! To forget for ever! My shame, my terrible torture. You're a cruel lot! I shall go away, and stay away for ever! I can't stand it any more!"

"Yes, be off with you!" cried Sergei across the raft, accentuating his exclamation with a loud and cynical curse. Then he seemed to shrink together, as if himself afraid of the terrible drama which was unfolding itself before him; drama, which he was now compelled to understand. . . .

"Hullo! There! I'm calling you! Are you deaf?" sounded up the river the voice of Silan. "What are you about there? What are you bawling about? Ahoy! Ahoy!"

It seemed as if Silan enjoyed shouting, and breaking the heavy silence of the river with his deep voice, full of strength and health. The cries succeeded each other, thrilling the warm, moist air, and seeming to crush down on Mitia's feeble form. He rose, and once more pressed his body against the steering pole. Sergei shouted in reply to the master with all his strength, and cursed him at the same time under his breath.

The two voices broke through and filled the silence of the night. Then they seemed to meet in one deep note like the sound of a great horn. Once more rising to shrillness, they floated in the air, gradually sank away—and were lost.

Silence reigned once more.

Through the cleft clouds, on the dark water the yellow splashes of moonlight fell, and after glittering a moment disappeared, swept away in the moist gloom.

The raft continued on its way down stream amid silence and darkness.

CHAPTER II

NEAR one of the forward poles stood Silan Petroff in a red shirt, open at the neck, showing his powerful throat and hairy chest, hard as an anvil. A thatch of gray hair fell over his forehead, under which laughed great black, warm eyes. His sleeves, turned up to the elbow, showed the veins standing out on his arms as they held the pole. Silan was leaning slightly forward, and looking watchfully ahead. Marka stood a few paces from him, glancing with a satisfied smile at the strong form of her lover. They were both silent and busy with their several thoughts. He was peering into the distance, and she followed the movements of his virile, bearded face.

"That must be a fisherman's fire," said he, turning toward her.

"It's all right; we're keeping on our course, Ouch!" And he puffed out a full, hot breath, and gave a powerful shove with his pole.

"Don't tire yourself Mashourka," he continued, watching her, as with her pole she made a skilful movement.

She was round and plump, with black, bright eyes and ruddy cheeks; barefooted, dressed only in a damp petticoat, which clung to her body, and showed the outline of her figure. She turned her face to Silan and, smiling pleasantly, said: "You take too much care of me; I'm all right!"

"I kiss you, but I don't take care of you," answered Silan, moving his shoulders.

"That's not good enough!" she replied, provokingly; and they both were silent, looking at each other with desiring eyes.

Under the rafts, the water gurgled musically. On the right bank, very far off, a cock crew. Swaying lightly under their feet, the raft floated on toward a point where the darkness dissolved into lighter tones, and the clouds took on themselves clearer shapes and less sombre hues.

"Silan Petrovitch, do you know what they were shouting about there? I know. I bet you I know. It was Mitia who was complaining about us to Sergei; and it was he who cried out with trouble, and Sergei was cursing us!"

Marka questioned anxiously Silan's face, which, after her words, became grim and coldly stubborn.

"Well!" shortly.

"Well, that's all!"

"If that's all, there was nothing to say."

"Don't get angry."

"Angry with you? I should like to be angry with you, but I can't."

"You love Marsha?" she whispered, coaxingly leaning toward him.

"You bet!" answered Silan, with emphasis, stretching out toward her his powerful arms. "Come now, don't tease me!"

She twisted her body with the movements of a cat, and once more leaned toward him.

"We shall upset the steering again," whispered he, kissing her face which burned under his lips.

"Shut up now! They can see us at the other end;" and motioning aft with her head, she struggled to free herself, but he held her more tightly still with one arm, and managed the pole with the other hand.

"They can see us? Let them see us. I spit on them all! I'm sinning, that's true; I know it; and shall have to answer for it to God; but still you never were his wife; you were free; you belonged to yourself. He's suffering, I know. And what about me? Is my position a pleasant one? It is true that you were not his wife; but all the same, with my position, how must I feel now? Is it not a dreadful sin before God? It is a sin! I know it all, and I've gone through everything! Because it's a thing worth doing! We love only once, and we may die any day. Oh! Marka! If I'd only waited a month before marrying you to Mitia, nothing of this would have happened. Directly after the death of Anfisa I would have sent my friends to propose for you, and all would have been right! Right before the law; without sin, without shame. That was my mistake, and this mistake will take away from me five or ten years of my life. Such a mistake as that makes an old man of one before one's time."

Silan Petroff spoke with decision, but quietly, while an expression of inflexible determination flashed from his face, giving him the appearance of a man who was ready then and there to fight and struggle for the right to love.

"Well, it's all right now; don't trouble yourself any more. We have talked about it more than once already," whispered Marka, freeing herself gently from his arms, and returning to her oar.

He began working his pole backward and forward, rapidly and energetically, as if he wished to get rid of the load that weighed on his breast, and cast a shadow over his fine face.

Day broke gradually.

The clouds, losing their density, crept slowly away on every side, as if reluctantly giving place to the sunlight. The surface of the river grew lighter, and took on it the cold gleam of polished steel.

"Not long ago he talked with me about it. 'Father,' he said, 'is it not a deadly shame for you, and for me? Give her up!' He meant *you*," explained Silan, and smiled. "'Give her up,' he said; 'return to the right path!' 'My dear son,' I said, 'go away if you want to save your skin! I shall tear you to pieces like a rotten rag! There will be nothing left of your great virtue! It's a sorrow to me to think that I'm your father! You puny wretch!' He trembled. 'Father,' he said, 'am I in the wrong?' 'You are,' I said, 'you whining cur, because you are in my way! You are,' I said, 'because you can't stand up for yourself! You lifeless, rotten carrion! If only,' I said, 'you were strong, one could kill you; but even that isn't possible! One pities you, poor, wretched creature!' He only wept. Oh, Marka! This sort of thing makes one good for nothing. Any one else would—would get their heads out of this noose as soon as possible, but we are in it, and we shall perhaps tighten it round each other's necks!"

"What do you mean?" said Marka, looking at him fearfully, as he stood there grim, strong and cold.

"Nothing! If he were to die! That's all. If he were to die—what a good thing it would be! Everything would be straight then! I would give all my land to your family, to make them shut their mouths; and we two might go to Siberia, or somewhere far away. They would ask, 'Who is she?' 'My wife! Do you understand?'

"We could get some sort of paper or document. We could open a shop somewhere in a village, and live. And we could expiate our sin before God. We could help other people to live, and they would help us to appease our consciences. Isn't that so, Marsha?"

"Yes," said she, with a deep sigh, closing her eyes as if in thought.

They remained silent for a while; the water murmured.

"He is sickly. He will, perhaps, die soon," said Silan after a time.

"Please God it may be soon!" said Marka, as if in prayer, and making the sign of the cross.

The rays of the spring sun broke through the clouds, and touched the water with rainbow and golden tints. At the breath of the wind all nature thrilled, quickened, and smiled. The blue sky between the clouds smiled back at the sun-warmed waters. The raft, moving on, left the clouds astern.

Gathering in a thick and heavy mass, they hung motionless, and dreaming over the bright river, as if seeking a way to escape from the ardent spring sun, which, rich in color and in joy, seemed the enemy of these symbols of winter tempests.

Ahead, the sky grew clearer and brighter, and the morning sun, powerless to warm, but dazzling bright as it glitters in early spring, rose stately and beautiful from the purple-gold waves of the river, and mounted higher and ever higher into the blue limpid sky. On the right showed the brown, high banks of the river, surmounted by green woods; on the left emerald green fields glittered with dew diamonds. In the air, floated the smell of the earth, of fresh springing grass, blended with the aromatic scent of a fir wood.

Sergei and Mitia stood as if rooted to their oars, but the expression on their faces could not be distinguished by those on the forward part of the raft.

Silan glanced at Marka.

She was cold. She leaned forward on her pole in a doubled-up attitude. She was looking ahead with dreaming eyes; and a mysterious, charming smile prayed on her lips—such a smile as makes even an ugly woman charming and desirable.

"Look ahead, lads! Ahoy! Ahoy!" hailed Silan, with all the force of his lungs, feeling a powerful pulse of energy and strength in his strong breast.

And all around seemed to tremble with his cry. The echo resounded long from the high banks on either side.

THE END

Printed in the United States
125561LV00002B/17/A